VAMPIRES ARE FOREVER

VAMPIRES CRAVE CURVES
BOOK ONE

AIDY AWARD

MEET VOND, JAMES VOND~

He likes his drinks dirty... and straight from the vein. But he would never shake them... he'd much rather lick them, bite them, suck them, taste their very essence of life.

So why is he craving chocolate cake???

Meet Vond, James Vond~

I am a soulless vampire, in service to the Vampire Intelligence Agency as their top black ops agent, protecting the immortal royals of Europe in a world of shadows and secrets. My life revolves around strategy, competition, and keeping our society safe.

Why in hellfire have I been assigned to escort this delicious, plus-size fashion designer to meet one of the Immortal Princesses? For a damn dress? I should be out stalking and destroying the hunters who seek to destroy anyone and anything immortal.

When I meet Rose, everything changes. She smells like rich chocolate cake, and I bet she tastes even better. Not that I'll ever find out. F*ck fated mates. I'd never ask her to share her soul with me. That would make me vulnerable and put her in danger.

But denying us both what we want doesn't keep her safe.

And I'll eat the faces off the ones who think they can touch her.

If you enjoy an angsty, grumpy hero and a quirky,

sunshiny heroine, with lot of action and spice, Join James and Rose in this thrilling tale of supernatural intrigue and unexpected romance between a protective vampire and his cute and curvy fated mate.

Copyright © 2023 by Aidy Award

All rights reserved.

No part of this book may be reproduced in any form or by any electronic or mechanical means, including information storage and retrieval systems, without written permission from the author, except for the use of brief quotations in a book review.

Cover by: Jacqueline Sweet

For all my curvy, plus-size, chunky, thick girls who loved Twilight and wondered if when you were turned into a vampire, if the supernatural beauty you'd develop would make you skinny.
It wouldn't.
Because you're already beautiful exactly the way you are.

And for Sean and Hopey who didn't laugh when I said "How about James Bond Vampires?"

And for my dad, who did laugh.

Serenity is not freedom from the storm, but peace amid the storm.

— ANONYMOUS

JAMES

Chillingham. Dark, dank, and where all the fun happened. I hadn't been back at Vampire Intelligence Agency's training headquarters in probably a couple hundred years. I was no newb.

But when Gabriel gave an order, I followed. It was even stranger that we were both here in the training simulation room. What did we have to train for? He was the team leader, and I was one of the most experienced operators on the squad. Probably some whim of an Immortal Royal.

He'd have to fill me in on it later. The room hummed with tension as we crouched behind a makeshift barricade, eyeing the holographic representations of cunning vampire hunters prowling just meters away.

"Three on the left, two on the right," I whispered, barely audibly even in the quiet room. The thrill of adrenaline rushed through my veins, and I used that to focus solely on devising a plan to outmaneuver our opponents.

"Got it," Gabriel replied, flashing his fangs in a confident grin. "Piece of cake."

I rolled my eyes at his cockiness. Gabriel and I were the team's odd couple–him, the charismatic leader who wore his confidence like a suit of armor, and me, the brooding strategist with a penchant for overthinking.

"Alright, we'll split up. You take the three on the left, and I'll handle the two on the right," I instructed.

"Roger that," Gabriel agreed, then paused for a moment. A mischievous glint sparkled in his eyes as he looked sidelong at me. "You know, if you'd get laid, maybe you wouldn't be so tense all the time."

Good try. He'd never try to throw me off my game in a live op. But here in the Castle, we were constantly competing for that top spot.

"Focus, Gabe." This exercise was being observed by the princess and he was trying to get in my head so I'd fuck up while he made himself look good, just for shits and giggles.

"Aw, come on, don't be like that," Gabriel chuckled. "We've got plenty of time to strategize how to get you laid before these amateur hunters figure out our location."

"You have a one-track fucking mind," I muttered, my lips curving into a wry smile.

"Hey, it's got at least three. Fucking, sucking, and blowing up bad guys. In that order."

That was a lie straight from the pits of hell. He cared about our team and keeping the immortal royals from getting their dumbasses murdered more than any woman or pint of blood. Both of us did. We'd both gone way longer than we should have without blood while on a mission so we could protect some king, queen, prince, princess, or someone else who couldn't keep themselves safe.

"Look," he twirled a dagger, spinning it up and down over his knuckles. "All I'm saying is that there's no shame in letting someone in, you know?"

It made my teeth ache that he was being both serious and teasing my ass at the same time. I clenched my jaw and flipped him off.

"Rooftop." Gabriel pointed out the hunters approaching to the left, putting me straight into mission focus.

"Got it." I tapped into my supernatural speed to scale the side of the building and take out the first simulated enemy.

I let just enough of the hunting frenzy push into my blood, awakening the beast within. This was only a simulation so I didn't need to go full on dark side.

Golden Boy and I faced off in the dimly lit training room, on the same team and yet still competing to be the star of the show at the same time. The rhythmic thud of our fists and feet against the padded walls filled the air, the ting of daggers flying at our faux opponents, punctuated by the occasional grunt or sharp exhale as we struck down our enemy. Our every movement was precise and calculated, a testament to our years of rigorous training at the Vampire Intelligence Agency.

The exercise raged on as if there was no end to the number of hunters lying in wait for us. This whole thing was designed to force us to take full advantage of our supernatural powers.

I was only half as old as Gabriel but had worked hard to develop almost as many tricks as he had.

I shifted into my bat form and swooped down right behind a pair of hunters, popping back into my full body to snap one's neck, and sink my teeth into the carotid artery of the other, ripping his throat out in a blink.

Gabriel's mind control didn't work in a simulation, but his ability to move so quickly he became practically invisible did. It was damn fun to watch him corral a group of the dumbasses, then run a circle around them so fast only another incredibly old vampire would see him slit their throats one by one. I barely caught his actions myself.

We worked in tandem to vanquish foe after foe. Our vampiric strength and agility make us a formidable force against our enemies. But Gabe wasn't wrong, this was a piece of cake.

Why were we even doing it?

"Come on, James," Gabriel teased, his grin broadening as he dodged a stream of stakes shot at him from crossbows. "You're getting slow in your old age."

"Old age?" I snorted. "You're the one who is as old as the godforsaken First Vampire, oh ancient one. I was just pacing myself, unlike your overeager self."

"Ah, is that what you call it?" Gabriel launched himself into a series of swift kicks that took out two of the hunters I was about to attack myself. "Speed up that slow-ass pace. And same goes for your love life too."

First fucking Vampire above, but he was an arse. "Shut the fuck up, Golden Boy. You can't fight and distract me at the same time."

"Hey, I can multitask," he replied with a wink, just

before pivoting and landing a solid punch to the chest of a hunter about to stab me with a quite poorly simulated carved stake. He ripped the man's heart out and tossed it over his shoulder. "Seriously, man, when are you going to let yourself be happy?"

"Enough," I growled, frustration bubbling within me. Gabriel meant well, but the thought of opening my heart and letting someone rip it out like he just did to that poor, pathetic simulation of a human? Nope. No. Not gonna happen.

"Bravo, agents." A commanding voice echoed through the room, halting our simulation. Gabriel and I turned to see the Immortal Princess standing at the entrance, her regal bearing demanding our full attention. Her eyes were the unfiltered golden glow of an Immortal Royal, unhidden in her true form and absolutely direct, no more hooded than the eye of a snake, and her skin was so perfect and pale it seemed to float above the white and gold dress that held it miraculously upright.

Fuck. Princess Mary of Orange.

I was beating the shit out of Gabe later for not telling me she was the one observing.

"Impressive work. Your skills have not gone unnoticed." Her voice was a sharp discordant note.

When she spoke, the words seemed to come from somewhere that was enormous and yet smaller than the back of our minds.

"Thank you, Your Highness," Gabriel and I said in unison, bowing our heads in respect.

She approached us, looking me up and down, measuring and weighing me with her eyes. I was used to being ignored by the Immortal Royals that we safeguarded. Her focused attention on me was disconcerting. Not that I thought I was lacking in any way. I knew how to do my duty and do it well. What the hell was she searching for so intently?

The silk of her sleeves caressed my arm as she brushed past, the softness of the fabric and the delicate scent of roses mixed with the musk of newly burned ashes imprinted on my skin. I was going to need a long shower to get rid of her.

"James, I have a special assignment for you," she announced, her gaze fixed on me in a way that required me to look her straight in the eye and hold it, so she knew I wasn't intimidated by her or her station. "I need you to escort a talented young human woman named Rose from America to Scotland for an important event I'm hosting."

She meant her birthday party. How was she hundreds of years old and still wanted lavish parties thrown in honor of a day no modern person even remembered? She'd faked her death hundreds of years ago to join the Immortal's underground society. Most humans had no idea who she even was, unless they were some kind of British monarchy history buff.

"A human?" Despite my disdain for her party being called an important event, my curiosity was piqued about why she would risk bringing a human woman among us. Even the immortals usually brooked the rules of secrecy.

What a pain in the ass this was going to be. I was a highly trained special ops elite agent. Why the fuck was I being put on human babysitting duty?

"Yes," the princess confirmed, eyeballing me as if she

expected me to protest. This was definitely another test. "She's a gifted fashion designer who has caught my eye. I believe her presence at this gathering will be mutually beneficial, but she requires protection during her journey and, of course, the utmost of discretion."

"Of course, Your Highness." I masked my surprise and disdain with curt professionalism.

I knew better than to question the will of the Immortal Princess, even if this was a poor use of my skills. Protecting her and her ilk was my sworn duty after all.

"Very well." The princess nodded. "You are to leave tomorrow morning. Do not let anything happen to her, James. She is important to our cause."

Was she now? That was either a ploy by the princess to eliminate questions about why she was bringing a human into our midst for her own gratification, or a hint at something well above my paygrade.

"Consider it done, Your Highness," Gabe interjected.

As the princess swept from the room, I turned back to Gabriel, who wore an amused grin.

"Looks like you're going to have some up-close and personal time with a lovely human." Gabriel waggled his eyebrows at me. "Better watch out, or she might just fall for you, and then what are you going to do?"

"You could have fucking said this was a dog and pony show for Princess Mary of Orange, you bloody asshole."

Gabriel flicked some simulated brains off his blood and guts covered BDUs. "I may enjoy fucking with you to no end, but I wouldn't have kept that from you. I didn't know. All I was told was we were going to be observed by an Immortal Royal who had an assignment, and to pick my best agent."

Even though he was the team leader, I wouldn't put it past any Immortal Royal to play games with us. It was stupid and juvenile.

"Do we even have a dossier on this human?" I suppressed the tiny flicker that there was something hinky about this mission. Why me and why a human woman?

"Nope." He narrowed his eyes to where Princess Mary had taken her leave. "And you'd better get your ass in gear."

Morning was only a few hours away and I had some prep and packing to do if I was going to be ready to escort a human woman all the way from the States.

I shucked my gear, returned it to the quartermaster, and found a package waiting for me from Fleming. He'd provided me with a week's supply of serum of sun. Shit. Humans and their damn daytime hours. I checked my watch. Yeah. I'd be in the US in the next five hours or so, and that put me there right in the middle of their day. I dowsed myself with one of the bottles and pocketed the others.

In minutes I was in my Aston Martin, racing away from the Castle and toward my flat. I didn't slow down until I was stood in front of my wardrobe, methodically selecting items for the trip. I couldn't shake the feeling this assignment was FUBAR before it even started.

I muttered to myself while throwing my go bag together, "You're an agent of VIA, fucker. Get the girl, get her to the princess, and get her back home safe. That's it. Stick to the plan."

I zipped up my duffle, the sound echoing through the minimalistic empty room. Then I grabbed a bottle of O-neg from the fridge and headed to the airstrip reserved for VIA special ops. The earlier I hit the air, the sooner I could do some research on this oh, so special, human woman. If I was right and she was nothing more than a princess's whim, I was going to be working double-time to keep both her safe and the secrecy of vampires and the Immortal Royals intact.

What a shit show.

ROSE

*G*iddy. More than that, giddying giddy giddiness that giddied. That was the only way to describe the caffeinated swirl of emotions flittering through my chest.

I walked through my fashion studio, the one I'd built with my grand-prize winnings from the Great Big Fashion Off, surrounded by mannequins donning my new series of creations.

Every which way you looked was filled by the chaos of my latest project - an extensive collection inspired by historical figures of feminine badassery. Intricate sketches of Queens like Elizabeth I and Liliʻuokalani adorned the walls, while fabric bolts and sewing machines cluttered the worktables.

Every inch of it had excitement bubbling up inside of me, but also the little niggle of worry that what I was creating wasn't going to be good enough. Exactly like when I worked on the designs I did during the show. This time there were no judges to give me a thumbs up.

I carefully adjusted the hem of a regal pantsuit inspired by the elegance of Marie Antoinette. I snipped some escaped strings from the floor-length tunic based on Boudica's rebellion, and smoothed a wrinkle from the front of a satin gown with fur trim that would have looked perfect on Ella Fitzgerald.

And as always, these samples from the collection were all plus-size. Rounded bellies and wide hips, thick thighs and bubble butts galore would be celebrated, not hidden, by my designs. A year ago, I fought hard for a tiny bit of notice for plus-size fashion and was sure I'd get eliminated in the early weeks of filming.

Since the show's live finale, I hadn't even had time to design and launch my first line because I'd been inundated with bespoke, high-end, couture orders from plus-size celebs, fat-positive influencers, and rich women around the world who embraced their luscious bodies and told diet culture and fatphobia to fuck off, just like I had... publicly, on national television... live... in prime time...very loudly.

But now that awards season was over, and I didn't have any more red-carpet dresses to create, I had one hot minute without a dozen new orders. My team and I had embraced the time to create my first line. The finished pieces were displayed around the room like a museum.

I walked from one to the next, and each piece I moved on to made me swoon all over again. Especially a daringly modern dress influenced by Cleopatra's legendary allure. I couldn't help but linger on the intricate beadwork, feeling a sense of kinship with these strong women of history.

"Ah, Cleopatra," I murmured to myself, "So powerful, woman, yet you allowed your heart lead you astray."

"Rose, is that one finished?" Anna, my newest assistant, pointed at the Cleopatra-inspired dress.

"Almost." I kind of didn't want to complete the final few dresses in the collection because the magic of making them would be over. Once they were done, I couldn't fiddle and make adjustments. There was no more deciding what was missing. "Just needs a few more touches."

"Who knew nerding out about history would come in so handy. It really shines through in this collection." Anna had that same swoony look in her eye admiring the collection as I felt. "The way you've brought these women to life... it's incredible."

The two of us had bonded over our love of weirdo history documentaries and famous women through the ages when she'd quoted Countess Báthory in her interview. I'd hired her on the spot.

"Thank you." I beamed. "There's just something about understanding the lives of those who came before us, you know?"

"Definitely." Anna nodded. "What can I do to help finish this one?"

"Got anymore gold thread hidden away?" Hand sewing all those beads ate up everything we had in stock. We should both knock off for the night, but I just wanted to finish a little bit more.

"I got you." Anna grinned and pulled out a box she'd clearly been keeping back for just such an emergency. It was like she could read my mind.

I loved everyone on my team, but Anna was the best hire I'd ever made. She didn't care about the accolades or the notice but got her satisfaction with feeling helpful and completing the projects, like it was her mission in life.

My fingers worked their magic, expertly weaving the golden thread and beads into the lines of the Cleopatra-inspired gown draped over my dress form. The lights of the Chicago skyline at night filtered through the tall windows of my studio, casting an interesting glow on the racks of luxurious fabrics and colorful sketches pinned to the walls.

"I'll just pop out and grab us some tasty beverages and snacks. I have a feeling this is going to be one of those long nights, eh?" Anna waved and let me get to my work. She and I were both night owls and that worked out great. I loved working after regular business hours because the phone stopped ringing, my phone quit pinging with notifications, and I could get lost in the work.

I didn't even notice the hours tick by after she returned, until the sun was actually starting to lighten the sky. "Speaking of powerful women," Anna slapped a magazine down on the worktable next to me, her tone shifting to mischief, "the article about you in Style Squawk just hit the stands."

"Oh, gimme. Did you read it yet?" I flipped through the pages to find the story. They'd interviewed me not long after the season finale of GBFO in a 'where are they now?' type thing.

"Yeah." She gave the magazine a side-eye. "They spent a lot more time speculating about your love life–or lack thereof—than your success."

I scoffed, feigning disinterest. "Ah, they did ask me like one whole question about whether I had a significant other. I guess they'll write anything for attention."

I shut the magazine and tossed it before I even found the article. I didn't need anyone or anything poking at any insecurities. The internet did enough of that, and I was well-practiced in ignoring the haters. "I don't have time for click-bait nonsense."

"Of course not," Anna agreed and shoved the trash can under the table and out of sight. "But umm, there really hasn't been anyone?"

I shrugged and threaded a bead onto the needle and thread. My love life, or lack thereof, wasn't up for discussion.

Anna didn't get the message. "It must be hard, right? Being so successful and accomplished, and yet still searching for that special someone?"

Why was she pushing this? While I felt a connection with her, we didn't actually know each other that well. Maybe it was her own insecurity about being a bigger girl coming through. I busied myself with adjusting the drape of the gown, getting back to work, waiting to see if she would too. "Oh, you know how it is. Love has a way of finding you when you least expect it, yada, yada."

"Sure," Anna replied casually. "You know, some dudes are probably just intimidated by a woman who's larger than life, both in her career and her physical presence."

I forced a chuckle. She wasn't the first to say something about how I was just too much for some people. That was on frickin' repeat in my life. "Well, if that's the case, those people aren't worth my time or yours anyway."

"Absolutely," Anna agreed, nodding vigorously. "You deserve someone who appreciates you for who you are, inside and out."

"Right. So do you." Now, if the rest of society was on board with that, I wouldn't be spending so many nights alone in my studio, would I? Ugh. That's why I didn't read trash about myself. I knew I was good, great even, just the way I was. But even I sometimes fell prey to the comments of trolls.

I turned my focus back to the dress. I'd much rather pay attention to how my designs were perceived than me. With each stitch and embellishment, I wove a piece of my heart into the fabric, creating something beautiful and timeless. No matter how much I put into it, something was off. It wasn't the design, it wasn't the fabric, and it was irritating me that I couldn't figure it out.

"Breakfast is here." Jorge, my longtime friend and now business manager, sing-songed his way into the studio, bearing gifts of chai tea lattes, egg bites, and cake pops. Starbucks breakfast at its finest. He knew exactly what I needed, and I loved him for his empathy and people skills that I mostly lacked. "And weirdly, we have snail mail. Check out this fancy schmancy envelope addressed to you, Rose."

The mysterious letter did indeed catch my attention. The wax seal, an actual seal and not some sticker, bore the emblem of what looked like a royal crest straight out of one of my history shows, piquing my curiosity. I carefully broke the seal and unfolded real parchment. Like, who wrote a letter on folded parchment?

"Dearest Rose," the letter read, "Your talent has not

gone unnoticed, and I believe you are the perfect candidate for this task. I am writing to formally invite you to design a dress for me to don at the upcoming celebration of my birthday. I shall send my guard to escort you to my castle one week from today. A workshop with everything you'll need will be ready and waiting for you. Sincerely, Mary O."

Jorge tapped the paper. "That's bit presumptuous of this Mary O. How does she even know you're available? You're in high demand. Does she even have the money to pay for the masterpiece you'll create for her?"

"Uh, she's sending her guard to escort me to her castle. I think she's got enough to pay me to design a dress." I'd already exchanged a few emails with this Mary, who was the opposite of contrary, even if not entirely forthcoming with who she was. All I got was that she was some kind of descendant of royalty in England and had, in fact, already paid a hefty down payment to have me make this dress for her.

Once I'd gotten the rest of the details ironed out with her, I would have forwarded her info onto Jorge to add to the schedule. Sometimes these crazy rich women expected me to jump when they said how high. I hadn't known she wanted me to come to her to do it. But there was no way I was missing out going to Europe to stay in a castle where actual history had been made.

"Uh, hold up." Jorge pointed to the top of the parchment page. "The date on the letter is a week ago today."

"Indeed," I murmured, my heart racing with excitement and trepidation. I stared at the elegant, looping words of the letter, a thousand ideas for a dress that would fit into my badass women of history line flying through my mind.

"Rose, you're not going, are you?" Anna made a face at the letter and shook her head like it was dirty.

"Of course I am." I hadn't admitted to anyone, not even really myself, how I'd missed the adrenaline of all that pressure the show put on us to design quickly and come up with something spectacular on demand.

I loved the new line we had right here in this room, but it was missing that something special and this last-minute opportunity was exactly what I needed to find that spark.

Jorge snapped his fingers. "I know that look. You are already there in your head. So, then, let's do this, babes." He had an all too familiar mischievous glint in his eye. "And, you know, if you happen to fall in love with the handsome bodyguard coming to whisk you off to this castle, then who are we to stand in your way."

"Shut up. How do you know he's handsome, or is a he for that matter?" Or that he'd be even vaguely interested in a girl with thighs that were probably thicker than his?

"It's called manifesting. Look it up." He gave me that ultimate *duh* look.

I rolled my eyes at him and grinned. "Well, that would add an interesting twist to the assignment."

"Exactly! So, let's get to work. You need to pack, and primp for your fairytale, uh, I mean your journey." Jorge clapped his hands once like that was all it took to make it so.

"Right," I agreed, determined to channel this new adrenaline rush into creativity.

"I'll just keep working on the bases of the other dresses while you're gone then." Anna stared at the letter like it was going to jump up and bite her.

I wasn't sure if she was mad at me, or disappointed that she couldn't go with, or what. This industry moved like there was no tomorrow, and she'd have to get more flexible if we were going to continue to make this work. I was glad to be seeing this side of her now rather than at something like New York Fashion Week. "That'd be great. I'm sure I can Zoom in if you've got questions or whatever. And I promise to bring you back some souvenirs. Maybe next time I can talk them into bringing the whole team."

"Uh, yeah." She flicked the letter and turned her back on me and Jorge, picking up the thread and beads I'd set down.

Jorge gave me a look that I understood immediately. He didn't even have to ask what her problem was. I'd deal with it when I got back.

He and I headed across the hall to my loft, and I shot an email off to Mary O. to let her know I was happy to accept her invitation, would love if she could let me know when to expect her guard, and any tips on what to bring she might have for me.

By the time Jorge had picked out about twelve outfits too many, and I'd packed some comfy clothes for working in and a couple of options to wear to the party if I got to go, I was starting to crash from staying up all night.

"You take a powernap and I'll wait for your Prince Charming."

"Shush your face. This isn't a blind date. It's a job and

the fee will pay half your salary for the year. So have a little respect, butthead." Instead of a nap, I grabbed my sketchbook to while away the time until the mysterious bodyguard showed up.

I set to work sketching out ideas for the gown, my fingers dancing across the paper as images of historical figures and luxurious fabrics filled my mind. Maybe, just maybe, I drew a couple of menswear ideas too. And they were not for some fairytale prince either.

Nope. These images were dark, luxurious, and sensual, and had my imagination going to places it shouldn't. I was blaming that one hundred percent on Jorge.

He took one look at the one I was working on and raised an eyebrow. "Hope you packed your vibrator."

JAMES

The moment I laid eyes on Rose, standing on her doorstep in a blood red dress that floated around her like a fucking dream, the universe tilted in a whole new direction. One that I was ill prepared for.

Which really pissed me off. This was no ordinary escort mission. A whole other set of rules would need to be applied to deal with this dressmaker and her humanity that I should have better prepared for. That was a mistake I wouldn't be making again.

I'd done what research I could on her and her known associates to make sure she had no connections to the threats to Mary O., the Royal Immortals in general, or the vampire hunters plaguing my kind for thousands of years. As far as I could tell in the short amount of time I had to dig into her and her past, she had no knowledge of the supernatural world. She hadn't even crossed paths with the dragons, wolves, or witches we kept tabs on in her area.

As soon as our eyes met, her very presence overwhelmed my senses. The scent of deep, rich, chocolate filled my nostrils, causing an almost unbearable surge of conflicting emotions. Need, hunger, and yet also intense protectiveness. It was impossible that she was a mere human with no Immortal or other supernatural ancestry, yet her captivating aura was undeniable. She was magical, without having access to a single bit of magic, elemental or otherwise.

She was utterly and simply human.

And I was a vampire.

She was prey.

I ignored every cell in my body and smiled politely.

Her intense gaze held mine as if she could see straight through me. I straightened my posture and extended my hand to her, getting on with the mission in the way I'd been instructed. Professional and nothing more. "Rose, I presume? I'm James. Mary O. sent me to fetch you. Pleasure to meet you."

She took my hand, and an electric sensation ran up my arm, leaving me stunned for a moment. Surely, she must have felt that too, but her expression remained courteous and businesslike, if a little curious. "Likewise. I'm excited about our journey to a real live castle so I can design a dress for the mysterious Mary O."

"Indeed," I replied, my eyes never leaving hers. "Ready to go? Can I take your bags?"

"I'm ready. Please, come in and I'll grab my stuff." Rose gestured for me to enter her home, completely unaware that the monster within me needed her invitation into her domain. It had been a long time since I'd interacted with a human anywhere that wasn't public, on Immortal Royal property, or my own turf.

I opened up all my senses, putting myself on high alert, and stepped across her threshold. The world around me filled with more color, more scents, more everything than I'd experienced in the last five-hundred years combined. The air was thick with the sweetness of dark, decadent dessert—a combination of sugar and spice that tickled my nose and made my lips turn up into a predatory smile. I licked my lips instinctually. My fangs dropped, prepared to take my prey down and drink the most decadent flavor of her blood.

My nostrils flared seeking out this tasty treat awaiting me, until I realized it was her.

Rose's scent, her mere presence, was intoxicating. I found myself wanting to drink her in like sweet nectar. I hadn't been hungry five minutes ago, and now I was dying for a drink of blood.

No, not just blood. Her blood. Only her blood.

I averted my eyes so she wouldn't see them darken and go red with need. For her.

It took me a full breath to retract my fangs so she wouldn't see what a danger to her I could be. What was I, fucking eighteen years old, needing restraint so that an innocent mortal didn't find out who and what I was? First Vampire save me.

"Thank you," I said, moving past her and trying to focus on the task at hand. I was no young and inexperienced vampire who couldn't control his cravings. I hadn't been hit with need this deep since I was less than a century old and still fighting for control of the beast I was born to be.

This journey was no longer solely about protecting her. Starting right now, it was about resisting the temptation that would slowly consume me.

"Is everything alright?" she asked. Her body radiated warmth like a roaring fire on a frigid night.

The perfect antidote for my cold, immortal lack of a soul.

"Fine." If I didn't quickly regain my composure, she'd either think I was a dumbass, or suspect me for what I truly was.

"Ooh, somebody is fine indeed. Dude is straight out of one of your sketches, and that accent. Yum." A young man, who smelled of absolute shite, joined us and looked me up and down.

From my research I knew him to be a longtime associate of hers, and her current business manager. He handed her a leather bag with a stylized R embroidered on the side, and matching rolling suitcase. "Good thing, I threw your, uh, thing we talked about, into your bag for you. You're gonna either need it, or well, either way, I hope it gets some good use."

"Shut. Up. Jorge," Rose said out of the side of her mouth and smiled at me. But I did not miss the way a blush rose up her throat and cheeks, turning her skin a delightful shade of pink.

Jorge looked between the two of us and grinned like an oracle with more secrets. If he didn't stink so bad, I'd eat him right here on the spot.

I scrambled for some kind of distraction. Something. Anything. "You have a lovely home, Rose."

At my innocuous compliment, Rose's heartbeat sped up. I could hear every damn beat calling to me. My fangs ached.

She looked around the room, her eyes lingering on a bookshelf filled with not just leather-bound volumes, but interesting items in between. "I got to spend a little bit of time and money lately finding just the right pieces from around the world to inspire me and my work."

She had art and books that could have adorned the walls of royalty. Ironic that.

"Your passion for history is evident," I said, noticing the titles of the countless biographies lining her shelves of people she knew as dead royalty, but who were in fact, my charges to guard and protect for all eternity.

We should absolutely be leaving her home and getting her on the way to Scotland and out of my charge as soon as possible. Yet here I was, chatting her up.

"I'm a bit of a history buff myself." If you counted actually living through the history she liked to read about. I was going to have to warn Princess Diana to update her look and even keep out of sight if she could. She hated these parties anyway, so maybe the VIA could convince her not to come at all. But probably not. The Council of Princesses did tend to stick together.

Even if Rose was an anglophile and history buff, it wasn't like she would recognize anyone.

Even the recently deceased Queen Elizabeth who'd decided she liked herself around the age of twenty-years old. A bit young if you asked me, but she had been quite wrinkly when she'd faked her death and finally retired to take her place among the Immortal Royals.

I thought she'd never give up the ghost. Charles hadn't either.

Most of the Royal Immortals chose to look around the modern equivalent of their mid-twenties to thirties. It wasn't like any ordinary human would recognize them in jeans and jumpers rather than gowns and codpieces.

"Really?" Her eyes lit up and I was so dead.

That smile would haunt me the rest of my life for its beauty.

"I suppose we'll have time to chat about that on the trip?" Her eyes lingered on me, yet she maintained a respectful distance. That was good. Incredibly good. The farther away I stayed from her scent, her heat, her beauty, the better.

But what the fuck was I going to do when she was mere inches from me in the car?

Be a professional. That's what. She was a human and couldn't know about vampires or the Immortal Royals, and so she was completely off limits.

Except to bed.

There were no rules about getting her naked, under me, and screaming my name as I made her come on my cock. Not as long as I made sure she didn't remember me afterwards.

No. No. I wasn't here to fuck her, and I certainly wasn't here to drink her blood and make her mine. I was here to escort her into a world of supernatural danger, protect her for her brief stay, and then return her home, untouched.

It would be easy to manipulate her memories though. We could have our way with each other, and she'd be none the wiser.

Bollocks. What the hell was wrong with me? Sure, I'd bedded many a beautiful human, even taken blood from some of my lovers because we both enjoyed it when I did, and then gave them memories of sweet dreams and nothing more.

I wasn't a fucking saint. My absent soul was evidence of that. But I was only a monster when I had to be. Dammit, why had Mary and Gabriel picked me for this mission? I would have happily remained unaware of this adorable American's entire existence if somebody didn't need a new fucking frock.

I cleared my throat and gestured back toward the door. "Shall we go?"

"Yep. I'm really excited to meet this Mary who sends hot bodyguards to—" she looked between me and Jorge with her mouth hanging open. "I'm blaming you for putting inappropriate thoughts into my head, Jorge. Just for that, you're on plant watering duty while I'm gone."

Jorge saluted us both with that damn grin. "You don't have any live plants. Now you two crazy kids get out of here, and Rose, have fun storming the castle."

"Ooh. You." She did not finish that sentence, but grabbed her bags and stomped to the door and held it open for me to follow.

I took the luggage from her and shut the door on her giggling, stinky friend.

When we entered the lift, I could finally breathe again. Even if every inhalation was heavy with her sweet scent. I counted the floors as we descended, telling myself I absolutely would not push that hold button to stop us long enough for me to press her up against the back wall, wrap her legs around my waist, and fuck us both blind.

"Have you known Mary O. for long?"

That put a damper on my libido. Thank fuck.

"Quite some time." My lips curled down into a small frown of their own accord, thinking about how Rose had no idea I meant literally hundreds of years. I had to forcibly reshape them into an undistinctive form. "She is... unique, to say the least."

"Unique. Right. Can't wait to meet her." She said that with genuine excitement that took me a little aback. It had been a long time since anyone I knew was happy to be in the presence of someone so demanding and downright bratty.

"Believe me, Rose, she has been eager for someone with your talent to design for her again."

The last was a French modiste who'd ended up in Henry VIII's bed, as so many, many women were wont to do.

Even the idea of Henry glancing at Rose had me clenching my teeth to hold back the red creeping into my vision. I'd kill him if he so much as touched her. The Immortal Royal's weaknesses would make it so easy to end his existence in the blink of an eye.

He might not age, or get sick, but I could slice off his head before he could say Church of England.

Except it was my sworn duty to keep the Royal Immortals alive and safe from harm. Even an ass like Henry. I just have to keep Rose well away from him because there was no way I was joining the ranks of the dark vampires who'd lost their way and weren't welcomed into supernatural society.

Bloody hell. Even the mere intrusion of thoughts like these were an unbelievably bad sign. The second we got to English soil, I was recusing myself from this mission. Gabriel could put the newb on this duty. What was his name? The one who'd ended up in the mud with the Baskerville's hound. Barely a hundred years old, and eager to make his mark in VIA.

This wasn't a matter of Immortal security. He could handle babysitting a human woman for a week while she made a dress.

Rage boiled in my throat. Again. The idea of the newb anywhere near Rose, and I was right back to seeing literal red. Fuck. Fuck a little rubber duck.

"You sure you're okay there, James? Sorry about what Jorge said back there. He's just being a butthead. I promise I am a solid professional and won't compromise—"

"Please accept my sincerest apology for making you think you've been anything less than perf... professional. I am merely concentrating on your safety."

"Oh. Umm. I'm not in any danger, am I?"

She had no idea.

ROSE

We stepped outside into the crisp morning air, and I watched James slide on his sunglasses like he was straight out of a James Bond movie. The British accent that melted my panties the second he opened his mouth, the tailored suit, the totally unnecessary but hot as hell protectiveness, all had me acting ridiculously swoony.

Jorge wasn't wrong when he'd said James could have walked off the pages of one of my sketches. He wore a drool-worthy tailored black suit with a black shirt, a shiny black tie, and a tiny pin on his lapel. The whole ensemble only served to accentuate his broad shoulders, beefy arms, and muscular legs. I'd never met anyone who looked so effortlessly perfect and also ready to pounce like a waiting predator.

Maybe it really was a good thing Jorge packed my vibrator because, if this guy didn't make a move to get in my pants, which I would entirely let him have access to, I was going to need it.

He led me to a really nice car, not that I knew anything about cars. But it was dark and shiny and had sleek lines that the designer in me could appreciate. No way it was a rental. James tossed my bags into the immaculately clean trunk like they weighed absolutely nothing. I watched those muscles flex, even through his suit, and internally giggled at how ridiculously handsome he was with the sunlight dancing around him.

Was his skin sparkling under the rays of the sun? No, dumb, silly. That was my lack of sleep talking. I clearly had sequins on the brain.

James opened the car door for me, his hand grazing my arm, which sent shivers across my skin just like when he shook my hand. Whoo boy, I'd better be a little more aware of where my body was because if we continued to brush up against each other, I'd be breaking out that vibrator in the plane's bathroom. I sat down in the softest leather seats I'd ever touched and reached to buckle my seatbelt.

When I turned back to snap it together, James was already sitting beside me in the driver's seat, staring.

His eyes lingered on... okay, I thought at first, he was staring at my boobs, but his gaze was firmly planted on my throat.

"Is there something on my neck?" I reached up to the spot his eyes were glued to and felt my own pulse going ku-thud thud thud. I was definitely that girl that always had food down the front of me or in my hair, so I would not put it past me to have a smear of cake pop chocolate on me and not have realized. Around his intense attention, I was feeling self-conscious.

"Nothing at all," he replied, shaking his head as if to clear it. "You look lovely."

"Oh. Thank you," I murmured, not exactly knowing how to respond to that unexpected compliment.

The fancy high-end engine hummed as we zipped up the road heading north, out of the city. He drove like a bat out of hell. His strong jaw clenched whenever he gripped the steering wheel to zip around someone going slower than we were, which was everyone, and his eyes were focused intently on the road.

He didn't say another word to me after that compliment, and I was not good at silence like that. "I thought we'd be headed to the airport. We can't drive all the way to Scotland."

Oh my God, I sounded inane.

"We use a private airstrip out of the city. Can't have you waiting around for a commercial flight and keeping Mary waiting."

"Right. Of course not."

I'd dealt with rich people, but this was next level. Security detail escort, private jet—what was next, champagne and caviar? "I've never been on a private plane before."

"You'll be quite comfortable, I assure you. Food and beverage service will be provided and there is a bed." He glanced over at me, and I swear to God, there was definitely an invitation in his eyes. "If you'd like to rest or... relax."

Relax. Right. That's what I wanted to do in a bed with hot bodyguard guy for the next few hours. Jeez. I needed to get my mind out of the gutter and not be acting so unprofessional right now.

It wasn't long before we were in the middle of nowhere, by which I mean practically in Wisconsin. This was farm country and not where I'd think a highfalutin airfield would be. We turned onto a dirt road, went through a tree lined stretch, and then, to my surprise, it opened up to a small airstrip with one of those 1940's looking army green hangars. You definitely wouldn't have any idea this was here if you weren't in know.

Everything was so secretive, and it made me feel like I was in a spy novel or something.

James pulled right up to the hangar and parked beside it. He hopped out immediately, then ducked down to look at me through the car door. "Ready?"

As I'll ever be. By the time I'd unbuckled and climbed out of the car, he had my bags in hand and waved to me toward the waiting steps up to a sleek black jet. The tail had those numbers and letters on it, but the side also had this round logo, all in black, and I wouldn't have seen it at all if the sun hadn't been hitting it exactly right.

There was a stylized bat with its wings outstretched in the middle. The bat was the same one as the pin on his lapel. Must be a company logo or something. Around the outside circling the bat was the Latin motto "Virtus, Infinitus, Aeternitas."

I stopped and stared, then looked over at James, narrowing my eyes at him, and then back at the jet. I hadn't checked his ID or asked any questions before I just up and walked out of my life with this dude. Was I being kidnapped and sold into some dark, mysterious human trafficking ring or something? "This is Mary O's jet? I didn't see her as a goth girlie."

Not like I had any idea what I was going to do if James was a bad guy. Kick him in the nuts and run for the car, I guess? Was a bit of a shame to harm the package I hadn't even gotten to drool over yet. I bet he had some big D energy going on behind those tailored trousers of his.

James crossed his hands in front of said package and cleared his throat. Shit. Oh, shit. I'd been staring at his crotch this whole time.

"This is V.I.A.'s jet. That is... my employer. We conduct security and other special operations for Mary O. and quite a few other affluent families in Britain. Now, if you please, the crew are ready and waiting."

Special ops? I assumed Mary O. had inherited her wealth from being a descendant of royalty, but now I wondered what exactly her family did that they needed special ops. Security, sure. Rich people are targets for all kinds of crazies, but now I really did feel like I was in a spy novel. Oooh, or if I was lucky, romantic suspense.

"What do those words mean?" I pointed to the logo.

He looked back at me as if he was surprised. "They translate to "Virtue, Infinity, Eternity" in English. Our motto. It's meant to convey a sense of boundless excellence, eternal virtue, and the everlasting nature of these values."

"Virtue, huh?" I gave him some side-eye, but I wasn't worried any longer.

He tipped his head and gave me what I could only refer to as a cheeky grin. "Yes, my lady."

"Ooh. I like that. Keep calling me that and you might just get lucky." I winked at him and sauntered toward the jet, appeased that I wasn't being kidnapped. No dark crime organization had a pat line about the everlasting nature of their values.

Besides, I trusted James. For no particular reason, he made me feel safe. Even if I probably shouldn't.

Another muscled guy in a suit stood at the top of the stairs and extended his hand out to me to help me up. James literally tossed my luggage to the guy, who had to scramble a bit to catch both the bags. "I've got her. You stow her items."

His voice had gone all gruff and snappish. Geez. Maybe he didn't care for his coworker? The other guy disappeared into the plane and James took the steps two at a time, replacing the offered hand with his own. "My lady."

We entered the jet, all decked out in more shiny black and leather, window shades all down, and lit only by lights above the plush seats. He directed me to one that was so far beyond premium first class, it belonged in an expensive club or the very masculine sitting room of a duke or a king.

"Do you have a seatbelt extender I can use?" I'd quit feeling embarrassed about asking when I flew commercial airlines. It wasn't like I was going to risk my safety because the tiny twenty-seven-inch seats didn't have belts long enough to go across my hips and belly. So, I certainly wasn't going to feel awkward about it on this fancy pants private jet.

"I think you'll find that the belts will fit you with plenty of room." His gaze wandered to my midsection and lingered on my hips.

"Miss, would you like champagne or another beverage

before we take off?" The other guy, who I guess was a flight attendant, smiled at me pleasantly.

What, no caviar?

"I said, I've got her," James growled through clenched teeth. I didn't miss his sneer at the other guy either, who raised his hands in surrender and retreated to the cockpit.

"James? Everything alright?" Like did he need his bipolar meds? Anger management classes? A good talking to by V.I.A's HR department about civility to coworkers?

"Of course," he replied, his voice steady and calm once again. He took the seat next me and reached across my lap, grabbing the buckle and snapping it together. I could smell the scent of his skin, which was clean, and yet reminded me of moonlight.

What did that even mean? I was being so gaga, like I'd never been around a hot guy before.

By the time he tugged the end of the strap so the belt was tight and low across my hips, I was breathing so fast, I was going to overdose on oxygen. See? Ga. Ga.

He glanced up at my eyes, then down to my mouth, and back up again. His tongue darted out and licked his upper lip, and I then forgot how to breathe. He turned and put his own belt on, leaving me to talk my lungs into working again.

"I apologize if I seemed overly curt. I am anxious for us to get in the air and on our way."

"Alright," I squeaked, pretending I hadn't just gotten completely turned on my alpha male bodyguard man strapping me down. "So, how long is the trip?"

"We'll be in Scotland around sundown."

That didn't actually answer my question, but it wasn't

like it mattered anyway. I was going to need a few hours to have a stern talking to with my libido before I met my new client if I didn't want to look like a teenager with overactive hormones.

We took off without incident, and once we were in the air for a bit, James got up and did bring me that glass of champagne. Also, some orange juice, an assortment of tiny pastries, and some kind of fancy yogurt with berries and granola on top.

I wasn't gonna say no to tiny pastries or a mimosa, and they were the perfect distraction from staring at him and counting his muscles. "Aren't you having any?"

"No, I, no. Thank you." He cleared his throat and swallowed like I was about to eat a feast and he was starving.

I was feeling pretty parched myself. "Fine. But you don't get to just sit there and watch me eat."

He didn't respond to that, but his eyes followed my hand as I popped something flakey and chocolate into my mouth and didn't stray as I chewed. I took another bite, really slowly, playing with the food just a little to see what he would do. Then I washed it down with a sip of the champagne, swallowing really, really slowly.

"Do you think I'll have anytime to do a little sightseeing? Any recommendations for some places nearby that I could visit? It's my first time across the pond."

He leaned back into the seat and stared up at the ceiling instead of me. I was still entirely tickled that he needed to distract himself from drooling over me. The good girl in me chastised the naughty side completely obsessed with wondering just how unprofessional it would be to have a whirlwind affair with one of my client's employees. Currently the good girl part was winning, but it was a close call.

"I believe Mary will want your full attention while you're preparing her garments for the party. But I am at your beck and call during your stay, so, should you have some free time, I would be happy to... arrange for a tour of the local sites."

"James," I breathed, my heart racing at the prospect. Of seeing the Scottish sights. Yeah, yeah. That's what had my internal organs doing the mambo. "That sounds incredible. I'd love that. It's a date."

He hummed his agreement, his voice low and sultry.

"Wait, no," I stammered, realizing the implications of what I had just said. "I mean, not a date–a professional outing."

What had I just told my libido about hormones and not looking like a fool in front of Mary O.? And I would if I thought I had a date with James for later. That's all I'd be thinking about. Not her dress, not my job, not my reputation.

A date.

With James.

At a Scottish castle.

"Of course," he replied smoothly, though a mischievous glint danced in his eyes. "Strictly professional."

Good girl Rose got in a death blow at naughty Rose after that gaff. I full well knew that if I impressed Mary O., I'd have all her family and friends coming to me for bespoke clothing too. That was too good of an opportunity to screw up because my mind was in the gutter, rolling around with a sexy-ass bodyguard.

I yawned and didn't even have to fake that I was tired so I could avoid flirting with James for the rest of the flight. "I think I'll nap for a bit so I'm wide-eyed and bushy tailed when we get to Scotland."

"Would you like me to show you the bedroom?"

Man, had I ever walked straight into that one. Because yes please. Ack. "No, no. This is fine. If I get into bed, I may never come out of there. I sleep like the dead. You don't need to hear me snore."

I pushed the little button to tip my seat back and turned my face toward the wall. At least that way James wouldn't see how hot my cheeks had gone. My exhaustion finally took hold and allowed me to escape from my ridiculous and slightly embarrassing attraction to James.

It felt like only a few minutes, but James gently shook my shoulder and said we were about to land. I had a lightweight blanket across me, and my chair had been reclined so my feet were up, and I was half prone. Geez, I hope I didn't slobber on this fancy leather.

Getting off the plane was much the same as getting on. Other guy pulled my luggage out from wherever it was stowed all this time, James bit his head off, other guy winked at me, James slugged him. You know, normal arrival stuff.

"James," I finally said after we'd gotten down the stairs and other guy had stayed in the plane, probably to ice his eye socket. "I know you take your job very seriously, but you don't need to protect me from every pair of wandering eyes."

"Forgive me," he replied, a flicker of vulnerability crossing his face. "Just doing my job, my lady."

Our eyes lingered on each other, and I felt as if we were both teetering on the edge of something dangerous and exhilarating. The connection between us was undeniable, but I had chosen to prioritize my job over my love life.

That's what I did. That's what got me ahead in my career.

"Rose…" His voice trailed off, and I glanced up to find him staring at me with an intensity that sent shivers down my spine. The last rays of the setting sun flickered in his eyes like a flame that neither of us could quench.

Without another word, he reached out and gently brushed a strand of hair from my face.

"James?" His name was nothing more than a breathless whisper, and I was unable to look away from his piercing gaze.

"Forgive me," he murmured, his lips hovering mere inches from mine. "But my resistance to you has worn thin and I need..."

Before I could react, he tilted my head back and pressed his lips to my throat. The sensation of his cool breath on my skin sent a shiver down my spine, and I gasped as he lingered over my pulse, taking in my scent. To my surprise, he gently nipped at my skin, just enough to make me feel alive in ways I never thought possible.

"James…" My voice trembled as I spoke his name, feeling the electric need between us grow stronger by the second. "We shouldn't… we can't…"

"I know," he whispered against my throat, his voice heavy with regret. "I'm sorry, Rose. I just couldn't help myself."

He straightened his spine, grabbed my bags, and pointed me to a waiting car. Oh crud. I wasn't going to be good at sitting next to him in such tight quarters again. I hoped this ride wasn't as long as the previous one in Chicago. Which was only like twenty minutes.

This time he opened the back door and I gratefully slid in. Just having those mere extra inches between us was going to help.

The sun dipped below the horizon, casting a warm golden glow over the Scottish landscape as we zipped along to our destination. The sight was breathtaking, and yet all I could focus on was the man in the seat in front of me, his strong profile silhouetted against the fading light. He glanced at me in the rear-view mirror, catching me staring, and I didn't look away like I should have.

"Beautiful, isn't it?" he asked, gesturing towards the castle I hadn't even seen popping up in the not-so-distant landscape because I was solely focused on James. "Welcome to *Caisteal Dubh Mhaothlinne*, more commonly known as the Black Castle of Moulin."

"Absolutely amazing," I agreed, my voice barely more than a whisper.

I was so screwed, and because I was choosing career over some straight up sexy times, I was not going to be screwed in the fun way.

JAMES

The ancient stone structure, normally hidden from human eyes by some ancient wards, loomed overhead, towering over us like the imposing guardian of secrets that it was. When I'd kissed her neck, I'd placed the charm on Rose's skin that allowed her to see through the wards.

I hadn't meant to let myself breathe her in. She smelled so damn delicious, and I'd been a half second away from sinking my fangs into that thick artery which was pumping her blood so close to the surface I could practically already taste it.

I was simply supposed to use the excuse of brushing her hair out of her way to deposit the charm on her. But that deep, rich, chocolatey scent of her blood called to me like a siren of need. I'd been smelling her arousal filling the confined space of the plane for hours and even the fresh air at dusk hadn't cleared either scent from my senses.

I couldn't let that happen again. I absolutely would maintain a professional distance from her for the rest of her stay. If I had to shove cotton wool up my nose, I would. The castle kitchen had better be stocked with plenty of O neg, because I was going to down every bottle they had and then some just to keep myself satiated around her.

We parked on the side, and I grabbed Rose's luggage and let her get out of the car herself, like an asshole. She stared at the grand entrance with the heavy wooden doors, and shivered, I imagined with excitement. I wanted her to shake and quiver because of my touch. Bollocks.

Like a fool, I placed my hand at the small of her back and escorted her through the doors, letting them creak shut behind us.

"Holy crap. It's a whole ass gothic castle." She gawked with awe and wonder, and I reveled in the adorableness of her introduction to my average, everyday world.

"Welcome to *Caisteal Dubh Mhaothlinne*," Gabriel said, appearing out of the shadows to greet us. He gave Rose his usual easygoing smile, but there was something off, it was evident in his tense stance. He wasn't even supposed to be here, and I'd expected a brigade of Mary's ladies in waiting to meet us and take Rose to her rooms.

I shot him a what-the-fuck-is-going-on glare and he almost imperceptibly shook his head and nodded toward Rose.

One of Mary's staff, one of the few humans who'd chosen the gift of long life and protection by the Immortal Royals in exchange for their service, finally came down the stairs to greet Rose and take her to her rooms. "Ms. Abernathy? We're so pleased to have you. Follow me, and I'll show you to your quarters. I'll be available for anything you need during your stay, at your security detail's discretion of course."

"Ohh, my quarters." Rose glanced at me with an impressed moue. "Exciting. Lead the way."

She went to grab her bag, but the staff woman stopped her with a shake of her head and a hand held out. "No, no. We'll have your bags brought up, miss. Please save your energy for attending Princess Mary."

"Princess?"

Ah, shite. None of us were used to having a human around who wasn't initiated and planning to stay. We'd need to have a chat with the staff and the guests to review the rules while Rose was here. This was the last fucking time we should allow one of Mary's whims to have a human around.

Gabriel jumped in to save the day. "Just something those of us working for her call her. You'll understand when you meet her, but keep that to yourself, duck."

"Gotcha." She made little finger guns at Gabriel, and I had to clench my fists not to move and stand between the two of them, so those fingers were aimed at me instead. My reward for that was her attention back on me, where I got a dazzling smile that would put all the modern toothpaste commercials to shame. "James, I'll see you later?"

"You will." I gave her a curt nod, trying my damndest to look like a fucking professional and not someone who wanted to follow her straight up to her rooms, shut the door, ravage her in the manner in which she deserved, and not come out for a week straight.

Once she was safely away, I faced Gabriel, whose friendly expression was replaced by a grim one. "Bad news, chap."

I knew it. "What?"

If there was a threat against Rose's safety, I was taking her out of here immediately if not sooner. And fuck me. That was unlikely. The threat would be against either us or the Immortal Royals. The hunters didn't care about anything but eliminating us from the face of the Earth. If anything, they'd try to recruit Rose to their cause.

She'd probably be better off with them than me.

"We intercepted some chatter. The hunters have caught wind of Mary's party and are planning to crash it. And, of course, there is no talking her out of holding it." Gabriel's words sent an unprecedented anger through me. As if I didn't have enough problems having Rose being surrounded by supernatural beings, now there was a threat from those absolute arseholes?

I was fighting to keep my emotions in check, which was far from my normal MO. "We need to ensure Rose's safety."

"Rose's? Not Mary's?"

Shit. "Both, of course, both."

Gabe shifted his full attention to me and that was rarely a good thing. "Something you want to tell me about?"

It took all I had in me not to visibly sigh. "Get Fleming here, now. I need him to work on a serum for me."

That got his attention. "What kind of serum? Were you

attacked? That should have been your lead. Those fucking hunters and their damned misguided mission."

I was going to have to tell him everything, wasn't I? "No. We didn't see hide nor hair of hunters. It's... Rose."

Gabriel frowned and crossed his arms. "The serum is for Rose? Why? What's wrong with her. You know it's against protocol to interfere with human lives. Unless you're planning on asking one of the Immortal Royals to invite her to join their staff. I gotta tell you, she doesn't seem the type."

Fuck. I did not want to have this conversation. But if I had to, Gabriel was the only one I'd consider confiding in.

"She's... my—" I couldn't say it out loud. Even thinking it felt dangerous.

Gabriel took one look at me, and he knew. Of course he did. "She's your fated mate. Bloody hell, man. We haven't had anyone on the teams find their Serenity in ages. I'd almost started to wonder if anyone else even would."

At least I didn't have to say it. "So, you'll call Fleming? Get him on this right away?"

"Sure, yes. Of course." Gabriel paced back and forth, using the motion to think. "I brought him with me. He's already here working to beef up the wards. What's wrong with her? Surely not something she'll die of in the next few days before you two bond."

Bond.

I thought Gabriel understood. He didn't, and I was fucked.

"There's nothing the matter with Rose. She's fucking perfect." Perfect mind, perfect smile, perfect ass. "But I can't bond with her. I cannot ask her to share her soul with me."

Gabriel looked at me like I'd grown a second and third head. "Make her your Serenity, and fuck everything else."

How did he not get it? Besides having to leave VIA? "Because it makes me vulnerable, and her a target."

I was not budging on this decision. It was the right thing to do. He frowned at me for a full minute. "Fine, but I think it's a mistake. Go ask him yourself. He's set up a makeshift lab in dungeon one."

Unable to shake the feeling of dread that settled in my chest, I double-timed it down the steps to the underground dungeons of the castle to seek out Fleming within the labyrinthine halls. I found him hunched over a table covered in vials and strange devices, his eyes hidden behind thick magnifying glasses.

"Ah, Vond," Fleming greeted me warmly, his nerdy enthusiasm palpable for whatever our missions needed—tech, serums, magic, or just about anything else. "What can I do for you? You didn't go through all that serum of sun I gave you already, did you?"

I'd worked with Fleming for my entire career. If I didn't trust him implicitly, I wouldn't be able to even mention Rose to him, much less explain this predicament we were in.

"I've got a delicate and special project I need your particular help on, and I'd like you to keep it as confidential as possible." I certainly didn't need all of VIA's special ops team knowing I was a liability. Especially not with the increased threat.

"I do, of course, have to report to Gabriel, and I believe

he passes everything up the chain of command to V, but aside from that, mum's the word as far as I'm concerned." Fleming's consistency in being a stickler for the rules was why he wasn't a field agent. But it also made him a damn good quartermaster.

But shit. I'd forgotten about V. Nobody ever saw the vampire who headed up all of VIA, except his assistant Eve. But if ever I was going to get dragged into his office, it would be for this.

"Look. Is there any way you can create a serum to stop a vampire's mating heat? " The vaguer I could be, the less would go in Fleming's report. The thought of putting Rose in even more danger by V finding out about us was unbearable. He was not known for having a fondness for VIA agents who fell in love.

Which I absolutely was not doing. I wanted to fuck Rose's brains out and let her do the same to me while I sipped on the sweet dessert of her blood. But I was not falling for the deliciously curvy, smart as a whip, funny, sassy, commanding woman. Nope. Never going to happen.

Fleming looked thoughtful for a moment, tapping his chin with his index finger. "It's a rather complicated request. I would need samples of blood from both the vampire and the person they were experiencing this heat with." His eyes flit about as if he was accessing the information in his brain file by file. "It would help if we had any previously mated agents and their Serenities to examine, but you know how V is. If you can get me those samples, I'll see what I can do though."

It wasn't policy for an agent to be fired once he mated,

but I didn't see any vampires and their Serenities hanging about HQ.

"Thanks, F, you're the best." If he could eliminate the intense attraction between Rose and I, maybe I could focus on keeping her safe from the looming threat of dumbass hunters.

"Of course," Fleming replied with a reassuring smile. "Anything for the upstanding field agents."

What about the not so upstanding ones?

Now, to get him that sample of Rose's blood.

Oh, fuck me twice. The very idea of Rose's blood just about laid me out flat. What the hell had I been thinking? I couldn't exactly ask Fleming to get it for me. I didn't want any other man or vampire near here for even a moment.

But I also did not trust myself to get it either. Perhaps I could just wait until she was asleep and sneak into her room... like a fucking serial murderer. If I was going to do this, I had better suck down every bottle of blood I could get my hands on.

I headed to the kitchen, stomped past the staff preparing real food for the Immortal Royals and their staff, and yanked the special cooler that held our sustenance open.

Gah. It reeked like someone had left a dead animal covered in shit that had been rotting in the sun for a week in there. I quickly grabbed the nearest bottle and slammed the door shut. The normally enticing red color looked off to me. Tentatively, I popped the lid and took a whiff.

Vampires didn't vomit, but if I could, now would be the time. The scent emanating from that bottle was pure poison. We'd been infiltrated and I had to be very careful with my next actions. The culprit was likely watching.

Gabriel walked in right at the moment I was about to dispose of the poison down the sink while feigning I'd already drunk it and was simply washing out the bottle for reuse. I waved him over and kept my voice low. "Those hunters are closer than we know. Smell this. I was about to be poisoned. We all were."

While any mortal poison wouldn't kill me, certain compounds could slow a vampire down and even incapacitate us, especially when we were also denied sustenance.

Gabe took a whiff, and then stuck his finger into the top of the rim, coating his finger with the tainted blood, before sticking it into his mouth. "Unless you're suddenly allergic to good old O-neg, I think you're smelling your upper lip. There's nothing wrong with this blood."

He took the bottle from me and downed it in a few gulps while I stood there gaping at him.

"What? I brought this in myself straight from the donor truck in Edinburgh this afternoon. And now I'm even more convinced you need to get your ass upstairs and find a way to explain to that lovely lady that she's in for the ride of her life."

"What the hell are you on about?" I wasn't going to like his answer, I just knew it.

"None but your mate's blood will you take, forever and always."

Fuck. Fuck. Fuck.

He'd just recited one of the lines from the Soul's

Serenity ritual that bonded a vampire to his one true mate.

"Nobody ever said it was because all other's blood smelled like the wrong end of a sheep's intestine. Are you seriously suggesting...?" I trailed off, unable to put words to the thought that had crossed my mind countless times since meeting Rose. The idea of mating with her and marking her mine was both enticing and terrifying.

"The bond between mates is powerful," Gabriel persisted. "It will not only provide her with protection but also give her the knowledge and strength to face any challenges that come her way."

What if V decided she poses a threat? What if he chose to eliminate her before she has a chance to learn the truth? "There's a reason interaction with humans is taboo. This is a shit show and you're no help."

I left the kitchen with Gabriel shaking his head at me. As far as friends went, he could suck a dog's bollocks.

Fine, I was going to have to get Rose's blood to Fleming sooner rather than later. I could go without blood for about as long as a human could go without water, a few days at most. But I would get lethargic, and downright stupid in the meantime.

I made my way through the castle, my footsteps echoing in the dimly lit hallways. The soft glow of candlelight flickered against the stone walls as I approached Rose's guest suite. I hesitated at the door, the scent of her already filling my nose and making my fangs ache for a taste of her. Swallowing hard, I raised my hand and knocked softly.

"Come in," Rose's voice called from within, sending a shiver down, down, down, to pool right below the belt.

I entered and found her sitting on an ornate chaise lounge, her dark curls spilling around her shoulders as she looked up from the sketchbook in her lap. Her eyes widened when she saw me, and a hint of a smile tugged at the corners of her mouth.

A smile I was about to destroy.

ROSE

The whole time I was sitting in my fancy pants suite waiting to be called in to meet Mary O., I should have been sketching up some ideas to show her. Was I? Nooo.

I was drawing James.

James in his suit, James in a tux, James in a t-shirt and jeans, James wearing nothing.

Can we say obsessed much?

Yes. Yes, we can.

I absolutely could not get the feeling of his lips on my neck out of my mind. I must have touched that exact spot about eleventy billion times in the last hour. It was probably red, and I should put some make up on it before I met Mary O.

Instead, I sat there like a bump on a white velvet log accented with gold inlaid wood and fluffy, furry pillows. And that's exactly how James found me a few minutes later.

When he knocked, I knew it was him without even seeing him. "Come in."

He appeared in the door, and it was all I could do to just sit there and smile instead of jumping up and tackling him so I could drag him to my bed and ride him like a cowgirl. Side-saddle of course, because I was a fucking lady, and we were at the castle of a princess.

"Rose." He said my name in a way that made my lower belly go all wonky and tingly, his voice way softer and alluring than any man's should be. "I thought this might brighten up your room a bit."

He pulled a single blood-red rose from behind his back. It might be cliche, but I loved roses. I was a bit surprised that he was bringing me a flower. We were supposed to be acting all professional with each other. Or at least pretending we were.

A flower, especially a single rose, from a man was the next level of flirting, if you asked me.

And I smacked good girl Rose upside the head and jumped in head over heels first to accept his invitation to the next step on the path to naked times. "It's beautiful."

I crossed to him and took the rose from him, all ready to inhale the familiar and sensual scent. My finger brushed against a thorn, which poked right into me and drew blood. I winced at the sharp sting.

"Ouch." I instinctively brought my finger to my lips to stop the bleeding, but James caught my wrist in his hand stopping me before I could suck on the wound.

Before I could protest, he gently pulled my hand close to his face, and for one ridiculously hot, and entirely too erotic moment, I thought he was going to put my finger in his own mouth.

I was woman enough to admit that I would have melted into a puddle of needy goo on the floor in a half a second if he had. Sadly, instead, he just examined my injured finger and blew cool air toward the wound. He grabbed a hanky out of his pocket, wrapping it around my finger and making a little red spot on the pristine white material. Who carries around a hanky? Hot British bodyguards, that's who. The pain seemed to fade away as we both stared at that blooming red.

"There you go, all better," he said, giving me a reassuring smile and dabbing at the last of the blood.

I couldn't help but feel a flutter in my stomach as I looked into his eyes. There was something magnetic about him, something I couldn't quite put my finger on. James had gone out of his way to bring me a rose, and that simple act had made me go even more gaga for him than before.

"I... thanks, umm..." Oops. I forgot how to talk because... was he leaning in? He was. Kiss me, kiss me, please, please kiss me for real this time.

His eyes locked on mine, and the intensity in his gaze sent a shiver across my skin, waking up every cell in my body so I could appreciate this kiss from my nose to my toes. His lips brushed against mine, and then he kissed me. The kiss was passionate, consuming, desperate, and it made me breathless and lightheaded. It was as if he was trying to communicate something through it, something he couldn't quite say out loud. The rest of the world fell away, leaving only James and me, locked in an embrace that I wanted to last forever.

He pulled me into his arms and dropped his lips to my throat once again. Something inside me screamed for him to bite me, to mark me.

Before I even finished that bizarro thought, he broke away and was halfway across the room. His back was to me, and his shoulders were heaving as if he needed to suck in all the air in the room just to keep himself in one piece.

"I shouldn't have done that. But I won't say I'm sorry."

I didn't even get to respond before he marched out the door and slammed it shut behind him.

Well, how do you like them ripe, round, apples? What the hell just happened? Maybe he'd get into trouble for dallying with me? I was going to find out. Right the fuck now, because no way he was leaving me with blue tubes.

Another knock sounded at my door, followed by the entrance of Mary O., her regal bearing filling the room.

"Rose Abernathy," she greeted me warmly, her eyes twinkling with kindness. "I hope you don't mind my intrusion, but I wanted to meet you myself, tonight, before we get started on the dress and all."

"Of course not." This was why I was here after all. Not to get up close and personal with a hot bodyguard. "I'm excited to finally get to meet you in person."

And check out the person who reigned over all this grandness, but who was so mysterious and secretive. Oh, and who needed a whole ass security detail who should have been underwear models, but who were hired to also protect me from some unknown threat.

"Likewise," she replied, her smile genuine. "How was your trip? I hope James has been taking care of you."

Uh, she totally said that as if taking care of me was an innuendo for, you know, taking care of me and my lady bits.

"He's been very professional and helpful." He had to have run into her out in the hallway. I was not going to be the one to get him in trouble. This had to be some kind of set up.

"Indeed," Mary's gaze went distant for a moment as some special kind of memories seemed to flicker across her face. "But enough about that for now." She waved a hand dismissively, her smile returning. "I'll let you get some rest so we can start nice and fresh tomorrow. But not too early, I'm a grump in the morning. Just let my girl know if you need anything, or, of course, James."

I swear to God, she waggled her eyebrows like she knew exactly what James and I had been up to in here just a few moments before and was encouraging it.

Rich people were so weird.

"Oh, and Rose. I wouldn't recommend wandering about the castle at night on your own. It's well known to be haunted. So don't fret if you hear strange shrieks or sounds. It's just your friendly neighborhood ghosties."

I waited until Mary closed the door behind her before looking up at the ceiling and laughing. What in the world had I gotten myself into? Okay, cool, cool. A haunted medieval castle. If that didn't give me some creative inspiration, I was clearly dead inside.

I opened up my suitcase and rummaged around for the soft but pretty jammies I packed and found them replaced with a dark red satin nightgown. Jorge. That rat.

After brushing my teeth and washing my face, I changed into it anyway, checked under the enormous bed for the previously mentioned ghosts, and crawled into the highest thread-count sheets I'd ever experienced in my life. I didn't think I was tired, but the next thing I knew, sunlight was streaming in through the window, the scent of coffee was coming all the way through my door where someone was knocking to be let in, and I was groggily coming out of some kind of a weird dream about sparkly vampires who drove James Bond cars.

"My lady," the staff member who'd showed me to my room yesterday, whose name I absolutely could not remember, poked her head into the room. "I took the liberty of making you a pot of coffee, seeing as you're American, but if you'd prefer tea, I brought a pot of English Breakfast as well."

She pushed her way into the room with a breakfast tray and came right over to the bed with it. I pulled the sheet up to my nose, checking real quick before I sat up to make sure this slinky lingerie hadn't caused any wardrobe mishaps in the night. Nobody needed to see a nipslip.

Except maybe James.

Ack. Stop it, naughty Rose brain.

"Thanks. You didn't have to do that. I can—"

"Oh, no. Mistress would have my head. Please allow me."

Okay, then. "I'd love to have the tea. When in Rome and all that."

She dropped two cubes of sugar and a good splash of

milk into a gorgeous teacup and then the hot tea on top. It smelled amazing.

"Here you are. I'll just lay out your clothes now, shall I? Might I recommend the soft white sweater and the linen trousers for today? You are meeting with the Council of Princesses, and they do love a bit of luxury.

She turned to an old-fashioned wardrobe and opened it. Inside, all my clothes were hanging on wooden hangers, with my socks, underwear, and bras folded and tucked into little shelves up the left-hand side. When in the world had she done that? I could have sworn everything was in my suitcase last night when I'd gotten ready for bed.

"I don't want to rush you, my lady, but it is almost noon, and Lady Mary will want to get started after luncheon."

"Noon? Cripes." I gulped my tea, which I expected to burn my tongue, but it was the perfect temperature, and threw back the covers.

"The sweater and linen pants will be fine. Thanks, uh, I'm so sorry, I've forgotten your name."

"No matter. Please, attend to your morning ablutions. I'll let Her Royal Highness Mary know you'll be ready in, say, a half an hour?"

"Yep, fine, good. Thirty minutes." I shut the door and hopped into the shower for the fastest rinse off in my life. Wouldn't do to be stinky when meeting... did she say the Council of Princesses? I hope they didn't expect me to curtsy and call them Your Highness, or Your Grace, or whatever. I may be a bit of a history buff, but I did not know royal rules of etiquette and the American in me kind of didn't want to. Silly little rebels that we were.

In precisely thirty minutes, lovely lady maid person whose name I still didn't know, came back to fetch me. I was ready with sketchbook in hand. I was not prepared for a room full of gorgeous, grand women to all squeal at the same time upon my entry.

Mary clapped her hands, and everyone quieted down. She came over and threaded her arm through mine and led me through a lavish drawing room adorned with gilded mirrors and fancy tapestries. We sat down on a chaise lounge with only room for us to sit amongst all its pillows. "Come, let's get to know each other better. We have so much to discuss and so little time."

"Of course. I'm ready and excited." That delicious bit of adrenaline from my reality TV show days flittered into my blood. Six days to create a kickass dress for her party. Let's do this.

"Allow me to introduce you to the Council of Princesses, or so we like to refer to ourselves. These are my dearest friends, some of whom I've known for ages, just ages." Mary said as she motioned around at the women. Seated at a long, elegantly set table were several women of varying ages, their eyes bright with curiosity as they turned to regard me. "That's Margaret, Caroline, Louisa, Maud, Diana..."

She said several more names, and they all sort of mashed together. I wasn't going to remember any of them. I'd have to ask staff lady to make me a cheat sheet, including her own name on it.

"So, this the infamous Rose, in the flesh?" asked one woman, her voice lilting with amusement.

"Indeed, it is," Mary squeezed my arm tighter in a way that felt kind of territorial. "Ladies, this is the talented designer who will be creating my gown for the upcoming celebration."

A murmur of approval rippled through the room as each woman stared at me, their expressions intrigued yet welcoming. As their eyes fell upon me, I felt the weight of their scrutiny, and I couldn't help but wonder what they saw in me to garner such interest. Maybe they were fans of the show?

"Tell us," another woman chimed in, her blue eyes focused on me intently. "How did you like James? He is quite fit, don't you think?"

"Di, be good, or I won't let her design for you next." Mary wagged her finger at the blonde.

Di folded her arms and pouted, but she had a mischievous glint in her eyes.

"We have much work to do, and little time to do it. Shall we get started?"

"Of course," I agreed, my excitement bubbling up inside me once more. With their encouragement, I quickly delved into a flurry of sketches and fabric swatches, my fingers dancing over silks, laces, and frills as I envisioned the perfect gown for Mary.

As I worked, I couldn't help but be overwhelmed by the sheer opulence surrounding me. From the priceless antiques to the sumptuous fabrics, the castle was a testament to wealth and luxury. Yet, oddly enough, despite my newish entry into the world of rich women who like couture dresses, I'd never heard of these women. Perhaps there were just a lot of people descended from royalty over here that just went about their daily business without being splashed across the papers like the Windsors tended to be.

As we finalized the ideas for the design, a crew of men brought in a couple of sewing machines, two surgers, a cutting table, several dress forms, which I noted were all plus-size, and bolts and bolts of fabric. A few of the women excused themselves, but several stayed and started unpacking the gear I'd be needing to make the dress.

"Oh, you don't need to do that. I can handle it all once we've finished." There was way more than I'd need here to make one dress.

"Didn't Mary mention? Several of us would like to stay and play. We'll make dresses to compliment what you've designed for Mary." The woman, who I think was called Margaret, smiled at me as she set up one of the sewing machines with a spool of white thread.

"Oops. Sorry, Rose. I hope that's okay." Mary wrinkled up her nose like a child who'd been caught with her hand in the cookie jar but knew she wouldn't get in trouble for it. "We don't get to have visitors like you all that often. This is a bit of a treat for us."

I noticed that the women who stayed were the ones who were on the plumper side, like me. Like I was going to say no to women who probably had just as hard a time finding beautiful clothes that fit like the rest of us plus size gals and had turned to making their own? No, I was not.

Never did I think I would feel like I related to a room

full of women whose haircuts probably cost more than my car. But in that moment, I suddenly felt like I'd just found my tribe.

"I love a busy sewing room. Bring it on." I met the eyes of each and every one of them to let them know I was sincere. "But I have one small question, and you'll laugh at me for not knowing, but who are you all?"

"Ah, that is a question many have asked," one woman replied with a mysterious smile. "We are simply friends who share a common bond, nothing more."

"Though our pasts may be intertwined in ways most unexpected," another added cryptically, her eyes flickering to the portraits lining the walls.

Glancing around the room, I noticed for the first time the eerie resemblances between the women seated before me and the regal figures depicted in the artwork hanging on the walls. It was uncanny, almost as if they were living, breathing doppelgängers of long-dead British royalty.

"Ancestors, perhaps?" I nodded toward the portraits, unable to shake the sense of déjà vu that suddenly gripped me. "You're all distant relatives or something?"

"Perhaps," the first woman echoed, her lips curled into a knowing smile. "Or perhaps there is more to our story than meets the eye."

"Indeed," Mary agreed, her gaze thoughtful as she studied my sketches. "But now is not the time for such discussions. We have much to accomplish, and the clock is ticking. Somebody call for tea, will you?"

I couldn't deny the thrill of belonging that surged through me as I lost myself in the creative process, surrounded by these enigmatic women who had welcomed me into their fold.

When the clock struck midnight, Mary O. declared us done for the day and weirdly insisted that she escort me back to my room. When we got to my door, I expected her to say something along the lines of splendid work or that was fun.

But she said the strangest thing to me. "Don't let fear stand in the way of your happiness, Rose. I know I did."

What? Like... what?

JAMES

Using every finely honed vampire and special ops skill I had at my disposal, I approached the sealed room, prepared to do some serious reconnoitering. I needed intel and could not trust anyone else to either gather it or keep the secrets I was about to overhear.

I flew silently in my bat form to perch just above the doorway, and then, with my claws gripping tight, I dropped my body to hang upside down. Yes, already I could hear the words filtering through the thick wooden door. I opened my senses, searching for the one voice I'd been assigned to know everything about.

"Gold is definitely your color, Mary. But we don't want you to look like an academy award statue. So, I suggest using it as an accent on the neck, wrists, and hemline."

Rose's words soaked into my mind and soothed an ache deep inside me. One taste of her lush red lips, the scent of her rich blood in my very hand, and I was an addict. Which is exactly why I'd stayed far away from her while she met with Mary and the other princesses. It had been one damn night and half a day, and I already wasn't sure I could control myself around her.

I'd nearly lost it last night. And from last night to this evening, I'd gone from hungry to frantically starving. Yet the supply of blood in the refrigerator still wreaked of shit laced with poison. In fact, all the human staff, and even the immortals staying here at the castle, smelled. The humans had surely all rolled around in a pig burrow, and the immortals vaguely reminded me of London of years past, reeking of urine and decay.

If I stayed here much longer, smelling the sweet treat of chocolate cake I knew to be Rose's blood, I may just break down the door and drag her away. It sounded as if they were wrapping up and I didn't want to be caught lurking outside the door, waiting for a glimpse of her.

I retreated from the room where Rose and the Council of Princesses were working on their designs, flying low along the plush carpet, feeling the heavy burden of not knowing what the hell I was supposed. I was firm in my stance not to ask her to share her soul with me and become my immortal mate. But without a taste of her blood, and if I were to guess, a steady supply of it after to keep me topped up, I would surely devolve into utter madness.

I'd never been that guy that talked through his problems, but this problem was too big, and the consequences affected too many. I already wasn't entirely thinking straight as it was. I needed to talk to someone who could understand the gravity of the situation, someone who would not judge me for my thoughts and emotions.

"James." Gabriel's voice snapped me so far out of my reverie that I literally fell out of my flight and had to take evasive maneuvers while retaking my vampire form, so I didn't fall on my ass in front of my friend and team leader. Because First Vampire knows, I'd never, ever hear the end of that. Gabe had fucking photographic evidence of my greatest gaffs since the invention of the camera. I think he had a whole museum of schadenfreude on his phone.

"Nice save, fly much?"

"Shut up." I paced, wondering just how much I should say to him. He was my friend, sure, but he was also my commanding officer, and could report me to V if he felt he had to. If I couldn't do my job.

Lesser vampires than me had been retired when their performance slipped. Lives were at stake, ones I had sworn to protect for all eternity. That had to be my priority.

"You need to take me off Rose's detail. I'm a more valuable asset in the field." I wasn't even sure how I'd ended up on fashion designer babysitting duty in the first place. I was a godforsaken trained killer.

"No can do. I didn't assign you this mission in the first place. This came from the top."

The top as in V? I'd assumed Mary O. had just called in a favor to get me. We may have a tumultuous past, but she trusted me, and I was the best, second only to Gabriel.

I ran a hand through my hair, frustrated as shit. "I can't concentrate on anything but Rose's safety. She's in the heart of our world now, and yet she knows nothing about it."

"Ah, yes, her safety. Right," Gabriel mused, his gaze

drifting towards the closed doors behind which the women were gathered. "I've been informed that the Council of Princesses are quite taken with her. It seems her talents have already earned their respect."

He was giving me an out, and I was taking it.

"Indeed." It wasn't my place, but I felt a swell of pride for Rose. She didn't belong in our world yet had already earned the admiration of the princesses. They didn't like anybody but their own, and more often than not, didn't even like each other. "But what if V decides she poses a threat? What if she finds out the truth, and he chooses to eliminate her?"

That was the reality of our jobs. Humans either joined the ranks of the few initiated, or they were taken out. This was how we'd maintained secrecy, even among the other supernaturals of the world, for so long.

"Vond," Fleming called out to us, his voice cracking with urgency as he rushed over to us. "I've run dozens of tests on the blood samples you provided and researched the issue thoroughly. I'm afraid there's no cure for your mating heat."

"I never said it was me, F." I don't know why I was trying to hide anything from either of them. One look at their faces told me I was being stupid not to count them as allies.

"Sorry, chap, didn't mean to out you. But it's not like I don't know the profile of every vampire on our team." He looked down at the file he'd brought along, filled with numbers and charts. "The bonding instinct is too powerful. Any attempt to tamper with it could have disastrous consequences. If you don't bond with Rose in the next, say, five or so days, you'll quite literally go feral. I've seen the breakdown of your cells already."

The weight of his findings crashed down on me like castle walls crumbling. I clenched my fists at my sides to keep from going absolutely ballistic. "There must be something you can do. A serum, a shot, a surgery?"

"Believe me, Vond, I wish there was," he replied, his eyes filled with genuine remorse. "The sooner you take her blood and get her to share her soul with you, the better."

My head dropped in defeat, and I struggled to accept the reality of our situation. Not only was Rose in danger from the hunters who wanted to destroy all immortals and the humans who associated with them, but she was also tied to me through an unbreakable bond. I had to find a way to protect her and keep my distance—a seemingly impossible task.

"Thank you for your efforts, F," I muttered, my gaze fixed on the floor. He and Gabe remained silent, understanding that there were no words to ease my pain.

"You'd better report this to V. I'll turn in my resignation after Mary's party." Putting an end to the only life I'd ever wanted.

"Fuck that." Gabe slapped my back. "You're the best operator I've got. I'm not losing you because you've found your Soul's Serenity. Let's see what happens when the two of you bond, and then see what V has to say. I have a feeling Ms. Primrose won't take kindly to him getting uppity about the first vampire in hundreds of years finding happiness."

If anyone would know what Ms. Primrose would think, it would be Gabe.

The discrete sound of the perimeter alarm pierced the air from the communicator on Gabriel's belt, shattering my momentary sulk. My senses sprang into alert mode as Gabe, and I rushed towards the nearest window. Peering through a crack in the shutters, we spotted two men in black clothing scaling the castle wall. We didn't hesitate. We were out the window and on the wall behind them before they could even reach the ramparts.

I scaled the wall and nearly caught the foot of the first intruder when he jumped onto the roof, turned immediately around and jumped from the top of the building, throwing his arms and legs wide. He was wearing a fucking flying squirrel suit, and glided across the garden instead of smashing his head in.

Gabriel and I watched the two men in black glide away and gave each other what-the-fuck looks. Something wasn't right. No hunters would give up so easily after infiltrating a vampire stronghold.

"What the hell?" I muttered, growing more suspicious by the minute. "This smells like a trap. They have to know we can easily fly along and capture them. Do we pursue?"

I could catch them in my bat form, but Gabriel's other form was even faster, and I'd bet money those hunters knew that.

Gabriel remained silent for a few moments before following my gaze back to the retreating figures. "No. This was too easy," he said finally, his voice low with suspicion. "They didn't even put up a fight when we confronted them. Just ran. Something else is going on here and they want us distracted and away from the castle. Let them go, and we'll track where they went later."

I'd never seen hunters act like this. We were about to turn and head back inside when I spotted something strange in the moonlight—a white piece of cloth fluttering in the breeze staked into the stone balustrade where they'd jumped. Curious, I motioned for Gabe to follow me as we crept closer for a better look.

When we reached it, we saw that it was a note written on parchment paper: "The Order knows who and what you are now—your time is running out."

This message was again, strange. Of course The Order knew who and what we were. They'd been hunting us for thousands of years. This was less like enemies had just infiltrated our stronghold and delivered us an ominous warning and more like someone pulling a prank.

"We need to heighten security around the castle," Gabe said, his confidence reassuring amidst the chaos. "No one gets anywhere near the wards without our knowledge."

"Agreed. Who can we bring in that can get here fast?" The whole of our Black Ops team would be my preference, and maybe some of the sods from over in VI5 or VI6 playing super-secret sneaky spies all night.

"Already taken care of. I've got a new trainee that arrived just before I found you skulking in the hallway." Gabriel led me to Fleming's makeshift lab in the dungeon again, where a young vampire leaned easily against the doorway as if waiting for nothing more than his drink to arrive.

"Silas Silvanus, this is Vond, James Vond." Gabriel introduced us with a flourish. "He's one of our most skilled operators and is on special assignment for Her Royal Highness Mary of Orange. You'll be helping him secure the castle."

"Pleasure, Vond." Silvanus gave me a small salute. "I've heard about some of your adventures with the Vampire Intelligence Agency. Looking forward to learning from the best."

This kid was suave. I half wanted to ask Gabe where he'd found him, a gentleman's club or straight out the pages of some romance novelist's book.

Oh, wait. Silvanus, as in one of VI6's greatest agents. Killed sometime in the last century. This kid was a VIA legacy, and one that Gabriel had been assigned to train himself. So far, all he'd done was get into some kind of mess with the Baskerville's hound.

"Right," I replied, offering a weak smile. "Let's focus on our mission and ensure everyone's safety. Sunrise is only a few minutes away, and I'd like to check on the perimeter and then our guest before we need to slather ourselves in F's serum of sun."

We set off to strengthen the castle's defenses. I didn't like that those hunters had been so close to Rose's room. Clearly just having me about wasn't enough to shield Rose from the dangers that lurked in the shadows.

But what if I did bond with her and ask her to share her soul with me? Anyone trying to harm her then would have to go through me, because I would eternally be by her side.

Why wasn't I at her side now?

And that was exactly why V didn't have mated agents

working in the Vampire Intelligence Agency. Hard to run black ops with a fragile human by your side.

The sun rose along the horizon, casting the castle into rays of burning light, the enormity of the task before me looming large. I wanted Rose so much it literally hurt. That dark, empty place inside where no soul resided, ached as if the darkness was seeping out and being burned up in the sunlight.

I couldn't bring myself to heed Fleming's directive, no matter how much I trusted him. The risk of revealing my true nature to Rose was too great, the potential consequences too dire. Instead, I resolved to find another way to protect her—a way that didn't involve breaking the bond of my duty or breaking her heart.

ROSE

The early morning sun streamed through the tall, stained-glass windows of the castle, casting a warm and colorful glow over the room. I sighed contentedly, savoring the peaceful solitude before the chaos of the day truly began.

"Rose, wake up! They're here!" Anna's voice rang out like a warning bell, shattering the tranquility of my room.

"Wha- who? Anna? Who is here? Why are you here?" My sleepy mind struggled to make sense of her words as I groggily pushed myself up from the bed. But I had no time to ask questions or even throw on a robe before the door burst open, revealing a group of men in ski masks.

Oh shit. This was why Mary O. had a security detail. I'd thought she was just overly cautious or had money to burn on hot bodyguards.

"Ah, Miss Rose," some creepy guy sneered, stepping into the room with an air of arrogance. "I'm afraid we have need of your... services."

Wait, they were here for me? Shouldn't they be trying

to kidnap Mary or one of her cousins-friends-long-lost-relatives who all looked like and were distantly related to the British nobility? They were the ones who would have ransom money. Jorge might have access to my business bank account, but I doubt my revolving line of credit was going to cover whatever crazy demand kidnappers would make.

Not that I wanted Mary to get kidnapped either but, come on. I wasn't royalty and I wasn't rich.

And where was James? He was supposed to be my bodyguard.

"Get away from me, asshat! I've got a... pillow, and I know how to use it." I jumped up and stood on the bed, shouting, trying to sound more confident than I felt. The fear coursing through my veins was nearly paralyzing, but I refused to let them see that.

"Such spunk," he mocked, grabbing hold of my arm and yanking me from the bed. "It'll make this all the more interesting."

"Please, don't hurt her!" Anna pleaded, her eyes wide with terror as she attempted to step between us.

"Stay out of this, girl," another one of the ski-masked men barked, pushing her aside, knocking her to the floor. Their eyes remained locked onto me, cold and calculating.

"My bodyguard will come for me." I spat right in my captor's eye, desperately clinging to the hope that I was being loud enough that James would hear and come to kick these guy's evil butts. "He won't let you get away with this."

"Ah, yes, James Vond, second-in-command of the Black Ops unit of the Vampire Intelligence Agency." I couldn't see his face, but I heard the leader's smirk in his voice. "It works out very nicely indeed that you're his whore."

"You can fuck the fuck right off with your whore-shaming." That's all I needed to find just a little more of that spunk he'd mocked me for. I shoved him right in the solar plexus with the heel of my palm, twisted when he groaned in pain and stomped on his instep, popped him right in the nose with my knuckles, and for my finale, went right for the nuts with my knee.

I didn't get to my coup de gras because it turns out, bad guys don't attack one at a time like in the movies. In a blink, two other guys were on me while Anna sat crying in the corner. How the hell had nobody heard the kerfuffle yet? Stupid old big castles with their giant stone walls and six-inch thick wooden doors.

Rough cords bit into my wrists and I struggled against my restraints. Asshat number one tried to drag me toward the door, but I dug my heels in hard and fought every which way I could, desperate to free myself.

"Come on, you stupid whore. Your vampire can't save you now."

Vampire? Oh shizznit. These guys were crazy pants. Great. Fine, I'd play into their psychosis.

"Yeah, he will, and he'll eat your faces off when he gets here. That sounds like an awful way to die, so you'd better let me go and fucking run."

The one who I'd socked in the nose, ostensibly the leader of the gang, grabbed me by the hair and tried again to drag me out the door. Anna trailed behind us on hands and knees, tears streaming down her eyes as she begged for them to let me go. She was quickly silenced by a foot to the face from one of the thugs. Ouch.

It hurt like hell, and I was going to need a good scalp massage, but I dropped to the floor like dead weight. "Pick this ass you, you assholes. Good luck trying to carry me down the stairs. I will fight you the whole damn way."

For once in my life, my big butt was working for me. This is why skinny chicks were the ones who got kidnapped.

He laughed in response and dragged me toward the door like a sack of potatoes.

My mind raced as we stepped outside into the chilly morning air. Where were they taking me? We were in the middle of nowhere Scotland. What did they want with me? They obviously knew who I was, and so they had to know I wasn't going to be good for any sort of ransom. I had so many questions, but no answers. All I could do was keep fighting until an opportunity presented itself to make my escape.

They drug me out a side door and across some gravel to some kind of catering van. So that was their cover. I skidded through the rocks the best I could to hopefully leave a trail for James to follow and figure out what happened.

But asshats number two and three went along behind and scraped over my tracks with rakes. Dammit, they were too fucking well prepared for this. Someone else from inside the van opened the doors and asshat leader shoved me inside. That's when I caught the scent of something that smelled a whole lot like what I imagined chloroform reeked of.

Yep, they pressed it over my mouth and nose. Unfortunately for me, that stuff also didn't work like in the movies. I didn't instantly pass out. But whoever was doing the chloroforming held the bit of cloth over my nose and mouth so tightly that I couldn't breathe.

I tried to gasp but couldn't, and dammit, I didn't want to die. But I did. I died. Dead. Doornail. Ding-dong.

Except I didn't think you could still get headaches in the afterlife. Nor did I believe said afterlife smelled so heavily of garlic. I blinked one eye open and then the other. Okay. Maybe the afterlife was garlic filled, because I was in a dimly lit room surrounded by more garlic than my Polish-Italian grandmother had used in her entire life. And Granny loved her garlic. "Grandma? Are you here?"

Good God. It just hit me. The yahoos who'd kidnapped me believed in vampires. I wasn't in the garlicky afterlife, I was in some kind of vampire-repellant safe room. It looked suspiciously like the inside of a restaurant's walk-in cooler. But a restaurant that only served garlic, because that's all that was in here.

Panic threatened to take over, but I couldn't give in—I had to stay strong. I knew James would come for me. It wasn't just because he was some kind of fancy bodyguard either. We had a connection, and I had to believe it would not only make me a priority to him but help him find me.

The door to the cooler popped open, and this time, my enemy wasn't hiding behind a mask. He looked me over and smiled all creepy and Snidely Whiplash like. "Ah, our lovely bait."

Bait? That was my first clue to why to took me. Bait for James? Crap that was bad. He would definitely come for me, and it was some kind of trap. If I could get this guy talking and learn a little bit more, maybe I could do something, anything, to warn James when he got here.

El Creepo entering the cramped space and knelt down beside me, fingering a bulb of garlic near my head. "Don't worry, whore. It won't be long before your precious vampire comes barreling in here to rescue you."

Sweet Jesus and Justice League. They were all delusional, which made them that much more dangerous. If they thought James was a vampire and I was bait to catch him, this was going to be way more of a clusterfuck than anything I could even imagine. "You're delusional. There is no such thing as vampires, dummy."

Probably not smart to call him names, but I was doing my best to hide my fear. If I could just buy some time, maybe I'd have a chance to escape.

Shoot. I should have pretended to be all surprised and on their side to win them over, and then I could have escaped. Dammit. Next time.

"Ah, how sweet. You don't know. I assure you, vampires are very real, and you were about to be the bride of one we've been trying to stake for such a very long time."

"It's maybe time to up your meds." Oops. There went another opportunity to feign fear of James and side with the leader of the looney bin. Probably not gonna happen now. I wasn't that sad about it. It was too damn creepy to pretend to be on this guy's side. "Once again. Vampires. Aren't. Real. You've been watching too much late-night TV. Oh, sorry, late-night telly."

"My family has been hunting the Immortal Royals and

their vampiric legions since the French Revolution. I've lost many a friend and good soldier of The Order to the bloodsuckers. I'll be all too happy to show you just how real vampires are and exactly how to kill one, if and when your paramour arrives."

"De. Loo. Shun. Al." I spelled his mental illness out for him because he clearly didn't know. "Also, you're breath stinks of garlic. Maybe invest in some toothbrushes and toothpaste before your next stay in the hospital with the plastic spoons and the nubby socks. Just saying."

He just smiled like crazy evil people tend to do. "Do let the guard know if you get hungry. The garlic bread here is to die for."

He turned on me and walked out, and in the brief moment the cooler door was open, I saw a glimpse of a restaurant kitchen. Aha. I was right. Now if only I had a way to let James know.

"Think, Rose, think," I muttered under my breath, wriggling my wrists in an attempt to loosen the ropes that bound me. Pain flared through my raw skin, but I pushed it aside, focusing on the possibility of escape.

"Almost... there," I whispered, feeling the knot finally give way. My hands were free. I quickly untied my ankles, then stood up and shook out my hands and feet to get the blood circulating again.

Very slowly, I depressed the button that opened the cooler door from the inside and opened it the tiniest of slivers. The kitchen was dark, and I surveyed the dimly lit room for an escape route, or a telephone. A small window beckoned, offering a glimpse at freedom. But oof. My shoulders and boobs wouldn't even fit through that thing, much less my hips and thighs.

Where was a good old-fashioned back door when you needed one? I crept toward the cafe doors that likely led toward the dining room.

"Rose," I heard the voice call out from behind the door seconds before it opened. Crazy McCrazypants Creepo stepped inside, his eyes widening as he saw me standing there, free from my restraints.

"Where do you think you're going?" he sneered, stalking towards me.

"Far away from here," I retorted, darting around him and running for the door. A strong hand gripped my arm and yanked me back, slamming me against the wall.

"Nice try," he snarled, his stinky breath hot on my face. "But you're not going anywhere."

"Let go of me." My voice trembled with fear and anger. The asshole only laughed in response, tightening his grip on my arm. "You're despicable."

"Perhaps," he conceded, his eyes gleaming with dark intent. "But I do so enjoy the game."

He shoved me back into the cooler and didn't bother to tie me up this time. I heard the locking mechanism click into place. Wasn't it illegal to have walk-in coolers that didn't open from the inside? What kind of vampire hunter, mafia bullshit restaurant skirted health and safety codes like that?

I pressed my ear to the door just to see if I could tell if El Creepo was still out there. I heard him discussing some twisted plan to stake James, but not kill him, and drain his blood like he'd drained so many others. Damn. I really was the bait to lure James into an insane trap—a delusional and deadly one. Fear gnawed at my insides, but I refused to let it consume me. James didn't deserve this, and neither did I.

I had no idea how to help James when he got here either. Maybe if I started howling and pretending I was shifting into a werewolf, they'd freak out long enough for James to take them out.

Right. That was a good plan.

Werewolf.

That's me.

JAMES

In the light of morning, after the intrusion by the hunters, I couldn't shake the feeling that something was off. What in the hell had they been up to? Gabriel and Silas went off to track the ones who we'd let escape so we could uncover their trap, but my senses buzzed with an underlying current of unease.

It was the sudden silence that alerted me to the fact that something was amiss.

I sprinted down the hallway, my vision going to red, my worst fears confirmed when I discovered the scene of chaos in her bedroom. Rose was gone.

The shattered remnants of Rose's bedroom door pushed an ice-cold rage through me. I let out an unholy, dark roar, the monster inside pushing to be released, to fight, to destroy. It took every bit of training I'd had from day one until right this second to reign my anger in and search for clues.

But make no mistake. When I found those who'd taken my Rose, they would suffer by my hand.

An open window. The scent of her fear lingered in the air, and the distant echo of her desperate cries haunted my thoughts. I clenched my fists, the anger and frustration coursing through me like a torrent.

While we'd been outside distracted by the hunters on the roof, someone else had been in the castle fucking kidnapping Rose. We hadn't taken the threats seriously enough. But who the hell wanted to steal my sweet, plump human?

"James?" Mary rushed into the room, looking as primped and polished as ever. I hadn't even thought to check on her. Fuck. I really was losing my mind to this mating need. There was no ignoring the waves of guilt and fear that threatened to overwhelm me, but I'd trained to suppress those kinds of emotions. Especially after the failed affair with Mary.

Locating Rose and ensuring her safe return, no matter the cost, had to be my only focus. I didn't care if it meant leaving Mary and the Council of Princesses here and unguarded. V could absolutely fire me, as long as Rose was safe.

"Did you see anything? Hear anything?" I snapped at her, not caring one wit about her station or my place.

"Oh no. What happened?" Mary's hands flew to her mouth, covering her shock and fear.

They were all going to die. I may have been on babysitting duty, but I was trained to be an absolutely lethal weapon. I methodically searched for clues to her whereabouts, determined to track her down and make her captors pay for daring to touch her.

I grabbed my communicator from my belt and barked

into it. "Code seven. I repeat, code seven. All agents report to the left wing, second-floor guest suite. Now."

Gabriel used a power that only the most ancient of vampires had mastered. Within seconds fog filtered into Rose's room through the window, and he appeared out of the mist. He glanced around the room, taking in the destruction, noting Mary's presence. Then he turned to me, and I saw the blood red in his eyes. He was almost as infuriated as I was. Almost. "Vond. Sit rep."

"Rose has been taken." I couldn't definitely say it was The Order, but I had no doubt we'd find proof of that pretty damn quick. I wanted nothing more than to dash out the front door and run after her, but I had failed her once already. I wasn't about to go off half-cocked, not knowing which direction to run.

No, this rescue mission would be calculated and deadly.

Fleming appeared a moment later, took one look at the room, and pulled out a scanner straight out of some sci-fi movie. Lights flashed, and the thing beeped and booped, and if F didn't give me some valuable information in the next naught point two seconds, I was going to smash the thing to bits.

"Noise suppressing ward, and strangely, a doppelganger charm, that must be how they snuck in undetected. But definitely humans. Three or four."

Fine. F could keep his gadgets intact.

Gabriel scowled. "They want to destroy all supernaturals, but happily use magic when it suits their purposes."

The Order. No ordinary vampire hunters. Humans whose lineage of terror against supernatural beings went all the way back to the Knights Templar. They feared and hated all immortals, supernaturals, and anyone who associated with us. The bane of our existence and the reason V had started the Vampire Intelligence Agency in the first place.

If they hurt a hair on Rose's head, her body, or even a fucking eyelash, I would be the vampire to destroy them.

Fleming put away his toy and continued his report. "Whoever they were, they were very good at covering their tracks. I didn't detect any blood, and it looks as if the lady put up one hell of a fight.

I knew Rose would be a fighter. When I got her back, she and I would do some official self-defense training. Not that I ever expected her to need to use it with me by her side. And it was when, not if. When I got her back.

"I can smell the aroma of her blood."

"You can?" Fleming took his machine back out and scanned in my direction. "I've got nothing."

"She smells like chocolate cake."

Gabriel, Fleming, and Mary all raised their eyebrows at that. I ignored them and followed my senses to track her trail as I should have done in the beginning. It didn't matter who'd taken her. I would kill them no matter what.

I followed her scent down the stairs and out a side door. The exit led to into the castle's courtyard which acted like a parking lot. I rushed outside and recoiled in the strong sunlight blanketing that side of the castle. Shit. One more smart move on the kidnappers' part.

I grabbed one of the vials of serum of sun Fleming had given me and dowsed myself in it. The shimmering coating it left on my skin would reflect the sun for a few hours, and I'd need every second I could get.

There, scuffed marks on the gravel, leading from the side of the castle. Someone had tried to cover them up. Sloppily and in a hurry if I had to guess. They knew Gabriel and I would only be preoccupied for a brief period of time.

"Silas here." Our communicators crackled. "I found an abandoned catering van, its doors ajar and the engine still warm. Looks like this was their escape vehicle, but the trail is cold from here. No scents at all."

"Gabriel. Put out an all points notice. They can't have gotten far." Gabriel nodded, and I knew full well he'd get grief from V for using our resources for this. Humans weren't our priority. Finding Rose wasn't either. Gabriel needed to make sure the Black Castle of Moulin went into lockdown, and all the immortals in, around, and nearby were secure. Rose was likely a ploy in a bigger plot to get to the Council of Princesses.

Until V redirected the resources for those duties, I'd use everything at my disposal. "Let me know if you get any hits. I'm going hunting." I wouldn't ask for more help than that. I may be ending my career, but the VIA black ops team needed their leader.

I began the hunt for the woman who I didn't want to mean so much to me, but who was rapidly becoming my entire world, by turning into my bat form. I could cover more ground that way, and any onlookers would assume I was some kind of bird.

Rose's chocolate scent led me straight to Silas, who was still examining the abandoned vehicle. I landed beside him, popping back into my vampire form so we could speak. "Have you found anything more?"

"No, sir. However, I was about to head toward the airfield and search there."

Fuck. Fuckity, fucking fuckballs. The car was indeed left less than a kilometer from our own damned airstrip. "How the hell had they gotten access without us even fucking noticing?"

"I may be new to the VIA, but it sounds like we've got a mole." Silas said that like he'd cracked the case. Perhaps he had.

I glared at him for a full minute, and to his credit, he didn't back down even a centimeter. If I hadn't known who his father was, I might suspect him. He was the newb. "I am assigning you the mission of finding out who betrayed us. You report your findings to no one except for me and Gabriel. Got it?"

He replied with only a simple nod. I'd better be able to fucking trust this kid. He was only a hundred years old, after all.

With this new insight, I had to be careful about using anymore of VIA's personnel or resources.

My supernatural speed got me to sprint to the airstrip in no time, following Rose's sweet aroma. But once there, I found exactly nothing. If they'd put Rose on a plane, even I wouldn't be able to track her scent. The plane she and I arrived in was hidden away in the hangar, and it wouldn't take me long to get her up into the air. I flew fast, but not as fast as the VIA jet.

The moment I walked into the hangar, it was obvious the culprits had been here. They might think they'd hidden their sabotage, but it took only a second glance to see that the jet had been tampered with. I slammed my fist through the metal nose of the plane.

If my communicator hadn't beeped, I might have torn the entire thing to shreds. "Vond. I just got a report from an agent in London. He reported known members of The Order taking an unconscious woman into a restaurant."

"Where?"

"I'm having him call you directly. Expect him now." Gabe hung up, and right on cue, my phone rang.

"Vond." The agent's voice crackled through the phone like we had a poor connection, interrupting my frantic pacing. "The restaurant is located at 61 Jermyn St, St. James's."

St. James, huh? Sus-fucking-spicious.

This whole thing had the flavor of some kind of personal vendetta against me and had nothing to do with the Royal Immortals at all. Sure, I'd offed plenty of Order zealots in my time. But this was war. I'd never heard of The Order putting hits out on any one vampire. They didn't even think of us as deserving of a name, much less individual attention.

"Thank you," I replied with renewed determination. With the location in hand, all that was left was to rescue Rose and put an end to this madness. Except, that wasn't it. There was something more nefarious afoot here.

"Be careful, Vond. Trust no one from here on out. Not only is The Order here, I've sensed the presence of other vampires."

I realized after they disconnected that I had no idea who that agent was and, of course, the call had come in from a secure unknown number. I relied on my instincts which told me from some place deeply seeded, that I could trust this intel and that warning. I'd have to check in with Gabriel later to find out who had broken the lead in this case. They knew as well as I did that this rescue mission wasn't going to be a walk in the park.

"Rose," I whispered, taking a moment to gather my thoughts and plan my next move. "Hold on just a little longer—I'm coming for you."

This was one of those times I wished I had Gabriel's gift of apperating anywhere he fucking wanted to. I'd be adding that skill to my training list when this was over. I didn't care if it took another five hundred years to master.

Since I didn't have that ability, I dowsed myself with a second vial of serum of sun, because this was going to be a long fucking flight.

I'd never flown so far, so fast in my centuries of life. But more than seven-hundred kilometers later, I was there. The late afternoon sun exhausted me, and I was badly in need of some sustenance. All the more reason to find Rose.

Because I wasn't denying myself her sweet blood any longer. Not if she agreed to share herself with me. If she didn't, well, I'd burn that bridge when I got to it.

"61 Jermyn St, St. James's" echoed in my mind as I approached the restaurant. The upscale yet old-world exterior radiated a deceptive air of innocence. I took a deep breath before entering, only to be assaulted by the overpowering scent of garlic. My senses reeled, and I struggled to maintain focus.

Yeah. The Order was here, and they knew I was coming. I couldn't smell for shit.

"Get a grip, James," I murmured to myself, shaken but determined. "You're here for Rose."

"Buonasera, signore," greeted the hostess, her eyes momentarily meeting mine before flickering away. I couldn't even smell her. Which was fine, she likely smelled like dog's ass. "Table for one?"

"Actually," I said, forcing a smile, "I'm just looking for someone."

"Of course," she replied with a knowing nod, turning her attention elsewhere.

I moved through the dining area, scanning the faces of the patrons while trying to ignore the discomfort caused by the garlic-saturated air. At last, I spotted a door leading to the back rooms. I knew I'd find Rose there, I just had to get past the vampire hunters staring back at me first.

ROSE

The cooler door popped open, and this time I was ready. I swung a heavy braid of garlic bulbs at my captor like a medieval mace and chain, minus the spiky bits. I missed him entirely and he stared at me like I was the crazy one.

"Your paramour is here, no doubt to rescue you. Are you sure you want to become his personal blood bank?"

Not this again.

I had to think fast. If James was actually here, my best chance of survival was to outwit El Creepo until he could get to me. I let him drag me out, but I knew exactly what I was looking for this time. I'd heard the kitchen starting to get busy, and nothing would throw a crazy kidnapper off his game like a good old-fashioned food fight.

I quickly grabbed a tray of spaghetti and meatballs as he led me past the line of prepared food, then hurled it at the other people back here who did not belong in a kitchen. Although, honestly, who were these chefs and cooks that none of them even blinked twice when a women dressed only in lingerie was dragged out of their walk-in cooler?

The spaghetti crashed against one dude's face, and that sent the rest of the baddies running in every direction. I guess they didn't like pasta. I felt a small surge of triumph as they dashed past me, their faces twisted in confusion.

Or was that fear? I mean, lots of people unjustly feared carbs, but...

James erupted into the kitchen, and damn, he was scary as all get out. Were his eyes red? Wait... were those fangs?

Clearly the garlic I'd been surrounded with was hallucinatory, and El Creepo's talk of vampires had gone to my head. Fine. Okay, whatever. I'd read my fair share of vampire romances and could play the part of the badass heroine.

I twisted out of El Creepo's grasp and dove for whatever Italian food was within my reach. A pot of boiling pasta, yep. As long as that wasn't holy water it was bubbling away in. I snagged a kitchen towel and snapped it at the nearest cook. "Run, dummies. That's a vampire, and he's gonna eat you up for dinner."

That totally wasn't how that worked. But I was working on the fly here. I grabbed the pot handle and gave the whole thing a toss toward wear El Creepo had been standing. Damn. He was gone. The water and pasta went flying, deterring anyone else from crossing my path. Good.

"James, over here." I grabbed a baguette with a lovely crispy crust to use as a bat and swing my way through the guys who hadn't run away like scaredy cats and were attacking James.

Good God. They literally held out crosses, and some of them had stakes. What a side show.

I couldn't see James, but I heard a lot of yelps and grunts and groans, none of which had his rich timbre to them. So, while it seemed like they were pushing him back out into the dining room, he was holding his own. That meant their focus was totally on him and not me.

This was my chance to get to his side so we could escape. I hit the guy closest to me over the head, cracking my baguette, and then slammed those crunchy sharp edges into his back.

"Ouch, lady. Watch where you're poking that thing. We're trying to save you." He turned on me and scowled.

"Wrong. You're trying to hurt my—" Uh oh. I'd almost called James my boyfriend. He wasn't my lover either, although after all this excitement, I was so jumping his bones. After the drugs wore off, of course. Safe, sane, and consensual. "My vampire."

I smacked the guy in the face with my trusty but broken baguette and sprinted toward the cafe doors.

As I made my way through the blood-splattered restaurant, I spotted James taking the high ground on a table. His eyes focused in on me and then he turned into a friggin bat.

A. Big. Ass. Vampire. Bat.

Okay, to be fair, I didn't know if it was a vampire bat. Didn't they eat fruit or something? Damn, these were some good garlic drugs.

Because of the whole bat situation, I was noticeably distracted, and accidentally dropped my baguette and stopped running to watch the James Vond Vampire Bat flying over everyone's head. But that gave some baddie a chance to grab me.

"Let go of me," I cried, struggling against the guy's too tight grip. To my surprise, he suddenly released me, his eyes wide with shock, and then his head fell off. Like, plop, oops, you lost your head. It even rolled a couple feet across the floor and went under a table. If I didn't know I was hallucinating all of this, I'd probably scream, or throw up, or both.

A second later, I felt someone else's arms wrapping around me from behind, gently but protectively.

"James," I breathed, relief flooding through me.

"Rose, are you all right?" His voice was deeper and darker than I remembered, and there was concern evident in his voice. But it was definitely my James.

"All the others are d-d-dead, aren't they?" I stammered and I think that meant shock was about to set in. "You should know now, before I go all catatonic on you, I've been drugged and am currently hallucinating that you're a vampire and the bad guys were vampire hunters with crosses and stakes and probably cooking their pasta in holy water."

James held me tighter and kissed the top of my head. "Right. We've got some things to talk about. But first, let's get the fuck out of here and someplace safe."

"Yes, please. Hopefully someplace with a shower, because I reek of garlic and if I never eat Italian food ever again it will be too soon." I was never eating Italian ever again. Although, anything with garlic sounded like a horrible idea. Maybe Scandinavian food? I didn't remember there being garlic in Swedish meatballs.

James laughed. "You do indeed smell of garlic. A sort of garlicky chocolate cake."

I didn't remember seeing chocolate cake. Tiramisu, yes. Chocolate cake, no. "Gross."

"Come, let's get out of here." He eyed the front of the restaurant and then tugged me toward the back. "I need to get you somewhere safe and call this in to VIA. We're gonna need one hell of a cleanup crew."

The kitchen was deserted, although there was still food cooking away. James cringed and squeezed my hand tighter when we skirted past the open cooler of garlic.

"James, wait," I whispered as we crept into dimly lit back room of the restaurant. "Do you hear that?"

"Stay behind me," he replied, his voice low and tense. My stomach did a flip flop as his protective instincts kicked in and he moved us closer to the source of the noise.

We peered around a corner to find El Creepo pacing, chastising one of his minions. He had the air of a desperate man who knew he'd lost control, and it sent shivers down my spine. I pushed my lips up against James's ear and whispered. "That's the guy who had me kidnapped and insisted you were a vampire."

"Then he needs to die." James did not whisper.

Shit.

"Ah, Vond," El Creepo said, smirking as he spotted us. "So nice of you to join our little party."

"Time to fucking die for kidnapping my Soul's Serenity, asshole." James's voice was crisp, calm, and oh, so deadly. "You should have stuck to hunting me and the Immortal Royals. This has nothing to do with her, and now you've made a personal enemy out of me."

"Ah, but it does," El Creepo responded, his grin widening. "You see, we received some very interesting information about you and your blood bride. And from a delightfully unlikely source."

Blood bride? I guess it was better than whore. Someone needed to teach this guy some manners. I had the distinct feeling James was about to do exactly that.

El Creepo rubbed his hands together like he was having fun. "Would you like to play a game to find out who?"

James released my hand, and gently pushed me a step back. "No."

Before I could even blink, James jumped the guy and was ripping El Creepo's throat out. With his teeth... fangs? The little minion who'd been standing there wide-eyed during this whole exchange peed his pants. Literally.

James grabbed him by the throat and held him up over his head. "Who me told The Order about Rose being my Serenity?"

Aww. I was his serenity? That sounded so peaceful and lovely. Must be a British saying.

More pee dribbled onto the floor and the minion burst into tears. "Please don't kill me. I'll tell you everything I know. Please, please."

James hissed at the guy. Was it weird that I was totally turned on by how utterly badass James was? "Who?"

"Another vampire. I don't know who he was, I swear. I swear. Please."

Ugh. More vampire shizz. When would these drugs wear off?

James growled. Like a lion or a tiger or a bear. "Rose, look away."

Ope. I spun. I wasn't sure why I couldn't watch him kill this guy in particular, but I was grateful James warned me when I heard a crunch and then something big and heavy flop to the ground. Twenty dead bad guys were enough for one day. Twenty-one was one too many.

Weird. Not a thing I ever thought I'd think about.

Strong arms wrapped around me once again, and this was definitely my new safe space. I spun in his arms and laid my head against his chest, letting him hold me for one entirely too long minute.

It was over. This whole nightmare was finished, and I wanted nothing more than a shower, a greasy meal, a really good roll in the hay with this man who'd saved me, and a week-long nap. Jorge and Anna weren't going to believe any of this.

I didn't even believe most of it.

He released me from the bear hug we'd been giving

each other, and then reached down behind my knees, put another arm behind my back, and picked me the fuck up.

"Holy crap. You can't carry me out of here. I'm far too big, and you've just been fighting the world's worst versions of Van Helsing's progeny."

"My sweet Rose. I will not only carry you out of here, as soon as we are at the safe house, I will also carry you to bed and ravish every square centimeter of your soft flesh. Don't for one second think you are too big for the likes of me."

Oh.

Swoon.

Or was that actually the shock setting in?

Nope. It was swooning, and I knew because shock does not make one's girly bits go all tingly and throbby. "Ravish me, huh?"

He replied with a small but devastating smile. "Something I've had a few centuries to perfect."

"Centuries... right," I muttered, my head spinning, trying to shake off the effects of the drugs. My mind was so damn creative with all this vampire stuff.

Except, the thing was, now that all the excitement of the battle was over, and the adrenaline rush was quickly baselining, I didn't feel like I was hallucinating.

Sure, James still had red eyes and pointy fangs, but where were the psychedelic trails? Where was the giant talking cockroach? Why weren't we fearful and loathing Las Vegas? And how come I could see quite clearly, and feel every single part of my body from my fingers to my toes and especially all the parts where James had his hands?

My heart pounded, just as it had a few moments ago, as I carefully eyed James. I put a hand up to his face, cupping his jaw. His skin was cool to the touch. Too cool for having been in a fight to the death.

He continued to make his way through the back of the restaurant and found the back door that had eluded me. I couldn't help it. I slid my thumb across his bottom lip, and then to the very tip of one of his fangs. It was sharp and punctured my skin. The tiniest bead of blood pooled, and James tipped his head back, closed his eyes, and took a long, shuddering breath.

"Rose. You shouldn't have done that."

JAMES

I snarled, fighting every instinct I had to sink my teeth into Rose's throat right now. The deep chocolate scent of her blood, right there in front of me, nearly turned me completely feral. I was hungry, starving, having been denied sustenance for far too long. Stronger, better, older vampires than me had turned dark side, giving into the monster within, for far less a temptation.

"I know what you are," Rose whispered.

A fucking monster.

"This is the part where you're supposed to tell me to say it. That's how it happened in the movie. But I don't really remember the rest of Kristen Stewart's lines. Something about skin as cold as ice or something?"

I dragged my gaze from that perfect, alluring drop of blood and up to her face. She should be very, very afraid right now.

Instead, she was... smiling?

No one ever smiled right before I sank my teeth into

their throat and drank them dry. They screamed, they cried, they passed out, they died. They didn't fucking smile so sweetly I could taste the sugar floating around her like a halo.

Not only did she smile, she brushed her mouth across mine, heartbreakingly soft, followed by a playful nip at my bottom lip. I froze, completely shocked out of the blood fever she'd incited in me.

Rose wiggled her plump ass to get down and I let her slide down my body, wanting to revel in the feel of her soft curves along my hard planes, but even that was beyond my brain's utter discombobulation. "You really are a vampire, and as soon as we get somewhere safe, with a bathtub and a bed, you're going to tell me all about that."

She took my hand and walked me out the back door and into the alleyway, like I was a lost puppy she was saving. That wasn't far from the truth.

Rose shook her head and mumbled something about hallucinogens and garlic and being silly.

"Rose. You should run. I am a monster, a real one. I've killed people, I drink their blood. Why are you not afraid?" And why had I not already sunk my teeth into her, taking what I needed?

"I know, I saw you rip several people's throats out tonight. Remember? But you would never hurt me. I know that all the way down to my soul. That's the only reason I'm not freaking out right now. I'm not much of a freaker-outer anyway, but you know what I mean—"

I grabbed her shoulders and spun her to look at me. Fuck, she was so damned beautiful. I meant to rail at her for being stupid, for not being afraid of me, but instead, I shoved her up against the back wall of the restaurant and claimed her mouth with mine.

Our lips crashed together, fueled by pent-up desire and the realization that we could no longer resist what lay between us. I cupped her face, using my thumbs to not so gently stroke her cheeks as our mouths moved over each other's, needing so much more than this.

The kiss was frantic and sensual, a turmoil of passion unleashed after days of holding back. Rose's heart thundered in her chest, her blood pulsing beneath her skin like an aphrodisiac.

But as suddenly as it began, I broke away, not trusting myself. I left her breathless and me desperate for more. "We can't do this here. You're not safe, and I won't claim you against a brick wall in a dirty London alleyway."

She ran a hand through her now disheveled hair, smoothing it, and then her dress, uh, nightgown? Fuck, I needed to find that safe place for her right now. And then we would talk. She deserved the truth—I owed her that much.

I might expire of thirst before I finished explaining the dangerous world she'd just become a part of, but my instincts screamed at me to protect her. Another part of me said to shield her from the darkness that lurked within me, but she was strong enough to handle it. I'd seen her face down a whole host of vampire hunters without flinching. If anyone could handle learning about the secrets of the supernatural world, it was my Rose.

Yes, my Rose. Mine.

And the reason I hadn't taken her blood, given in to

the temptation to drink her until there was nothing left, became so clear. She trusted me.

Fate trusted me to take care of her, and her of me. She was truly my Soul's Serenity.

"Come, let's get you that bathtub and bed." I took her hand this time and led her back out to busy Piccadilly. We came out just down the street from the restaurant, and it would never cease to surprise me just how oblivious humans were to what was happening around them. A few of the customers that had been frightened out of the restaurant milled about, but life continued on all around them.

I walked up to a small group huddled nearby and waved my hand in front of their faces, capturing their attention. In another breath of a moment, I had them mesmerized. "You decided not to eat at Franco's tonight, and instead had a lovely evening over at the London Eye where you grabbed sandwiches at the little coffee shop on the corner."

Rose stared agape at the group, and then made a face at me that I read as she couldn't believe I was doing this. In for a pence, in for a pound.

I snagged the phone out of the nearest lad's hand, held it up to his face to unlock, and quickly found his internet browser. Within a minute, I logged in to one of the popular vacation rental sites via an app, booked a place for tonight, and once again used his face to approve the charge to his credit card. I had the confirmation sent his email, opened that up, memorized the access information and also noted his name and address so he could be reimbursed later.

"Good, now pop on down to the tube and head to this young man's house. Stay there tonight and resume your regular lives in the morning, remembering only the fun you had at the Eye, and none of the incident here, nor any of the people you saw." The Piccadilly Circus stop was just up the block and based on the young man's identity that I'd just temporarily stolen, they'd likely gotten here on that line in the first place.

Rose popped into my instructions. "And feel free to have a wild monkey sex orgy when you get home, if that suits you all."

I had no idea if that idea would take hold in their minds. "You're a cheeky minx, Rose."

"You're just now figuring that out? Did you not watch Great Big Fashion Off?" She grinned at me, and it was now even more imperative that we have that talk and get to that bed to have a wild monkey sex orgy of our own. If that suited her.

"I did not, but I will add it to my queue as soon as possible." I did not actually have a queue, nor a telly. But for Rose, I'd get one.

The rental I'd arranged was a luxury one bed flat just off Haymarket and Orange a few blocks away. But Rose wasn't wearing any shoes and was only dressed in her silky nightgown. No way I was letting her walk like that. "Do you trust me, Rose?"

"Yes, but why are you asking?"

We stepped into the shadows, I wrapped her in my arms and transformed into my bat form. The magic of the shift brought her along too, like a babe I carried beneath me. She clung tight to my claws, and I took off into the night.

Only two minutes later, we landed right in front of the entrance, which was smashed between a sushi restaurant and a coffee shop. I transformed again into my vampire form and Rose squealed, still holding me tight.

"That was the weirdest thing that has ever happened to me, and I have so many questions."

"Of course, love," I replied softly, meeting her gaze. "Let's get inside, showered, and you can ask me anything you want to know over a nice cup of tea."

I punched in the code for the door and shut it behind us, feeling a modicum of safety for the moment.

Rose didn't wait even a moment to begin a barrage of questions. "Can you even drink tea? Like do you eat or do you only drink blood?"

I searched the flat and headed us straight for the shower. "I can both eat and drink like a human, but it offers me no sustenance. However, there is a deeper value in a good cup of tea."

No bathtub as she'd requested, but the shower stall was definitely big enough for two. The sooner I could scrub the scent of garlic from her, the sooner I could ravish her. I reached in and turned the water to scalding hot.

Rose only barely seemed to notice. "How long have you been a vampire?"

"Nearly six centuries," I answered, watching as she absorbed this information. "Vampires can either be born, or they can be made by a human being turned. I was turned when I was in my late twenties. That is a story for another time, but I've spent most of my time since then working for what is now known as the Vampire Intelligence Agency."

There were plenty of soft fluffy towels and a row of containers with body wash, shampoo, and conditioner. It had been a long time since I'd washed a woman's hair for her. She was right, I should have found a place with a big claw-footed tub.

"Ooh. V.I.A. Nice cover with that motto." Rose barely took a breath before she asked her next set of questions. "So, what's it like being a vampire? I mean, how does it work? Like, are you actually allergic to garlic, does holy water burn you, does it give you a headache if I say something like Oh my God? What about crosses, do you sleep in a coffin?"

Her last question had her eyes going wide. I used that to my advantage and stripped off my shirt for those eyes only.

"Alright, love." The soft glow of lights in the steam filled room played across her face, casting delicate shadows that highlighted her beauty even more. "I'll tell you everything you want to know and more, when you're naked and in this shower with me."

She glanced at the steaming hot water and tipped her head to the side as if just noticing it for the first time. "If we're getting in there together, you'd better give me the basic rundown first, because once we're naked, I'm going to forget every single question I have."

"First off, we have heightened senses—smell, hearing, sight. We can hear a heartbeat from a mile away and see in complete darkness." I paused, considering how best to explain our abilities without frightening her. "We're also incredibly fast and strong."

"Wow," she breathed, clearly fascinated. I couldn't help but smile at her enthusiasm. "But, um, are there any weaknesses?"

"Of course," I replied, my voice gentle. "Sunlight is our most obvious weakness. It burns our skin, and prolonged exposure can be fatal. We're also vulnerable to certain materials like silver and wood. A wooden stake through the heart will kill us instantly."

"Really?" Her eyes widened with surprise. "I always thought that was just a myth."

"Many myths are rooted in truth," I explained. "And the most important thing..." I hesitated, not sure how she'd react to this revelation. "We really do need blood to survive."

She looked thoughtful. "So, do you have to... hurt people to get it?"

"Most vampires take precautions not to harm humans," I assured her. "We drink from willing donors, but the VIA has our own blood banks." I left out the part about always erasing a human's mind after drinking from them.

"Okay, that makes sense," she nodded, looking relieved.

"Any more questions?" I asked, wanting her to feel comfortable with all aspects of this new reality, but I also wanted very badly to get her naked.

"Um, yeah. Can vampires have... relationships? Like, normal ones?"

"Our relationships are intense and passionate," I

admitted, feeling a heat rise in me as I recalled the kisses she and I had already shared. "We can love deeply, but there's always an element of danger."

Rose looked at me, her expression a mix of curiosity and determination. I could see her mind racing, processing all this new information.

The soft glow of the antique lamp illuminated Rose's face, making her eyes sparkle with curiosity. I could feel her warm hand still holding mine, and I knew that it was time to tell her the rest.

"Rose," I began, choosing my words carefully. "There's something else you need to know about vampires—about us, you and I."

"Us?" she echoed, her brow furrowing.

"Vampires can have fated mates, or as we call it, a Soul's Serenity," I explained, feeling my heart pounding in my chest. "It's a rare, powerful connection between two individuals who are destined to complete each other."

Her eyes widened slightly, but she didn't pull away. Instead, she leaned closer, intrigued. "And you think... I'm your Serenity?"

"I do," I admitted, my voice barely above a whisper. "I've never felt this way before, Rose. The moment I met you, I knew it was you. I tried to deny it, to protect you, but each day I wait, drives me closer to the brink of becoming a dark vampire, uncontrollable and uncaring about anything but my next drink of blood."

She looked down at our intertwined hands, seemingly lost in thought. I couldn't help but notice how perfectly they fit together—a testament to our bond, perhaps. But would she accept it?

"James," she said at last, her voice wavering. "A few hours ago, I didn't even believe in vampires, and now... now, you're telling me we're destined to be together?"

"The choice is yours." It was always hers. "If you choose not to be my Serenity, I will turn myself into V, the leader of VIA and he will... take care of things."

He would likely drive a stake through my heart and chop of my head. He may still do that. He was not a fan of fated mates.

A silence stretched between us, the weight of the decision heavy in the air. I could practically hear the gears in her mind turning, working through the implications of what I'd told her.

"Okay," she said finally, looking up to meet my gaze. "I can't deny how strongly I feel about you, even if it's something I don't fully understand. Life is about taking risks, and the scariest ones are also the ones with the greatest reward. Love is a risk, being with you is too, but it's one I'm willing to take."

"Are you sure?" I asked, wanting to give her every opportunity to change her mind.

"Absolutely," she replied, determination shining in her eyes. "I trust you, and if being your Serenity means accepting this new world, then I have only one more question for you."

Please let it truly be the last.

"Why aren't we naked yet?"

I had trained thousands of hours to utilize my vampire super speed for King and country. Never before had I put it to such good use. In less than a second both Rose and I were completely naked, and our clothing had been flung out into the hallway. The most glorious set of breasts I'd ever had the privilege of seeing called to me to be touched, caressed, worshipped, and most definitely sucked.

I didn't know how it was going to work, and I certainly didn't know why we were on this collision course to each other, but none of that mattered as much as having her in my arms and kissing her.

I kissed Rose and dragged her into the shower. Our tongues clashed, our teeth clacked, and I slammed into the wet wall, taking the blow to my back first and then turned to press her body against it, trapping her body against it with mine.

Rose shoved her hands into my hair and held me tight to her as our mouths mashed together under the wet spray. "I can't get enough of you. I want to taste you everywhere."

My mouth was watering wanting to taste more of her everywhere, and my need took over. I shoved her hands over her head and slid one of her nipples into my mouth and sucked like it was the sweetest of desserts. She groaned and threw her head back. "Ooh. Yes. But that's not showing me what good you can do with your dick."

I popped her nipple out of my mouth. "Patience."

"If you say it's a virtue and make me wait, I might scream."

"I'd rather hear you moan some more." I moved her wrists together and took them in one hand, freeing my other to wander. I had no intention of making either of us wait. I simply needed to ensure she was ready. I returned my mouth to her nipple, squeezing and pinching the other one. When she was moaning again, I moved my hand lower and between her thick thighs. I was going to get lost between her legs and enjoy every minute of it.

She was already wet for me, and my fingers slid between her folds easily. I pushed two fingers into her and found the sensitive nub of her clit with my thumb. Her gasped, incoherent mumble was all I needed to know I'd hit the jackpot. She twerked her hips forward, riding my fingers, and wasn't that the fucking hottest thing I'd ever seen. "That's it, flower. Take your pleasure. Let me see you come."

I needed her as close to her climax as possible when I took her blood.

She was melting in my arms and her nipples went from pliant and soft to stiff little peaks. Her moans were music, rising in pitch, crescendoing as she got closer to her orgasm.

At her moans that irresistible urge deep inside me, a hunger that demanded to be satisfied, reawakened. My vampiric senses recognized the vitality and sweetness of Rose's blood, pulsing just beneath her skin. If we were to truly become one, I needed to share with her my most primal need—to drink her blood.

"When we bond, I will take your blood. It's a deeply intimate act, and I would never take this step without your consent."

I could see the wheels turning in her mind, even as her body begged to come. With a determined glint in her eyes, she spoke, "I offer myself to you willingly."

Her bravery struck me like a bolt of lightning, making me fall even more in love with her. It was a rare thing for a human to trust a vampire so completely, and I knew then that our connection was something truly special.

I circled her clit again and again with one hand, and with the other, I gently tilted her chin upwards, exposing the delicate curve of her neck. I felt her tremble slightly beneath my touch. But it wasn't fear that caused her shiver. It was anticipation, desire, and trust.

"Are you ready?" I whispered into her ear, my breath sending tingles down her spine. She nodded, her eyes meeting mine with unwavering determination.

I closed my eyes and allowed my fangs to extend, feeling their razor-sharp points grazing my lower lip. This would send her over the edge into orgasm, and I wanted to taste every bit of her pleasure. With a tenderness borne from the depths of our bond, I pressed my lips to her neck and let my fangs sink into her flesh.

Her blood filled my mouth, and I was overcome by the sweetness and warmth that flowed between us. It was as if I were drinking in her very essence, becoming one with her in a way that transcended mere physical contact. The connection we shared deepened, solidifying our bond and taking the first step in truly sealing our destinies together.

"James," she moaned, her voice barely audible but filled with desire as she tumbled over the edge into her orgasm. Her cunt clenched around my fingers, the rhythm there matching the pulses of her warm blood flow into my mouth.

The intimacy of sharing such a deeply personal act with Rose was unlike anything I had ever experienced before. Her fingers threaded through my hair, holding me close to her neck as our breathing grew heavy and synchronized.

I slowly withdrew my fangs from her neck, licking the puncture marks gently to help them heal, and pulled my fingers from her swollen and wet cunt. I looked into her eyes, now filled with a fire that matched the one burning within me.

ROSE

James growled low in his throat and licked upwards along my neck to swirl his tongue against the shell of my ear, the vibrations tickling against my hairline. "I love hearing my name on your lips, and it's only going to get better when you're screaming it over and over again for all of London to hear when you come on my cock."

"Is super stamina also a trait of vampires?" While I was feeling all lovely and floaty from that full body orgasm his bite and thrown me into, I also really wanted the full Monty. I wanted him inside of me, and until he was, it was strange, but I felt like there was a part of me missing.

"Indeed, it is. We need no sleep, and I did warn you that a relationship with a vampire was intense. I won't stop until you're begging me to."

That wasn't happening anytime soon. "Then take me to bed or lose me forever, Goose."

"You got it, duck."

Oh no. He really didn't watch TV. Maybe because they

didn't have televisions when he was born almost six hundred years ago? That little fact was still mind boggling. I'd waded my way through accepting that vampires were real and all, but probably I'd have a little freak out later. In private.

I was down for dating an older man. But this was going a little crazy.

James turned off the shower and in the most ridiculous and cave man way, picked me up and threw me halfway over his shoulder, giving my butt a smack. Since his was right in my line of sight, I did the same.

This time I did not protest being picked up and carried. It was hot when I thought he was just a muscle-bound bodyguard. But now, since he'd said vampires had super strength, I was going to enjoy being carried around whenever and wherever.

He grabbed a couple of towels from a warming rack on the wall. Europeans were so smart. I was going to have to get me one of those. Then he marched down the only other hall, to where the bedroom must be.

With a quick toss, he got the towels over the plush duvet cover, so we didn't get the whole bed wet. Yet. And tossed me down next. I giggled, until he climbed over me, and our lips met yet again in a searing kiss, fueled by the powerful connection we shared.

I would never get enough of his kisses.

As our bodies pressed together, every touch seemed to amplify the bond between us. His hands wandered all over my curves, and I relished his touch. His mouth followed.

A moan slipped out as he kissed and licked his way

down my body, as if he couldn't get enough of me. More than a few times, I'd felt like I was too much for the men I'd been with. Not with James.

His fangs slid across the tight flesh of my nipple, sending spirals of need through my whole body. My hips rose against his hands, seeking out his touch to soothe the growing need there. But his teasing fingers remained light, elusively slipping away from where I ached for him.

"James," I murmured, twisting my hips toward his sly hands. "Don't tease me so."

His teeth nipped at my nipple, and I arched upward, pressing into the stinging bite, then the hot laving of his tongue that followed. His gaze lifted from my breast, and the feral look in his eyes stole whatever remained of my breath. "Hush, love. I know what you need, and I'm going to be the only one who gives it to you."

His tongue glided down along my ribs, and his hot breath blew against my navel. His grip on my thighs was just rough enough to turn me on, and he slowly, ever so slowly, moved his teasing kisses closer to my soaking pussy. It had been months, years, ages since we started this naughty game, and all I was getting was some deeply sexy kissing along the fold of my belly and sides of my thighs instead of deep and dirty between them.

"More. Faster. Damn it, I've seen you move faster than the air itself, so why are you going so slow now?" I huffed out a frustrated breath as I tried again to press myself against his teasing mouth.

He looked up at me again, his eyes steely and dangerous. "For that, I'll make sure to keep this as slow as I can. I'm going to take my time with you, and if you're a good girl for me, I might eventually let you come all over my face."

"Yes, let's skip to the coming part." If he made me wait very much longer, I'd be a puddle of need on the floor. I know I'd just had an orgasm to end all orgasms like two minutes ago, but all it had done was make me want him more.

"Hmm, or maybe I'll take you to the edge and then make you wait to come on these fingers." He raised one eyebrow, testing me, waiting to see how I reacted to his dominance.

I freaking loved it. Guys never talked to me this way. I didn't even know I wanted them to. I was always the boss, most of the time that carried over to the bedroom. With James, I didn't have to be. I could let him take charge and enjoy myself instead of having to take care of everything.

Need swirled around and around in my lower belly until that, and his words were all I could focus on. "Or if you're a very naughty girl, I'll have to skip licking your hot cunt and make you come on my thick cock. Would you like that?"

My entire body quaked with the possibilities coming out of his filthy mouth. There was only one answer that would work in my favor here. "I'm afraid I'm very naughty."

I wasn't. I was needy. While I very much wanted him to do all the delicious licking and tasting, I was desperate to have him inside of me.

"Ah, you are, and for that, I'm making you wait until you've come again before I fuck you." He looked me straight in the eye, testing how far he could push our game.

Damn. Busted.

I returned his stare, not breaking eye contact for a second. "Then make me come."

He chuckled. "You do have quite the naughty cheek. Don't even think about coming until I tell you to."

He continued his vicious stinging bites from my knee to the inner crease of my thigh, slowly, so slowly. He carefully crossed from one thigh to the other, all without touching any of the hot, wet, aching territory that I was very indelicately trying to shove toward his teasing mouth.

I moaned and groaned and whimpered, dying for him to taste me, to put his lips where I needed them most. Because the sooner I let him make me come with his mouth, the sooner I could be coming on his cock.

"Hush, my sweet. I'm definitely going to savor every second of tasting you, but not until you really want this as much as I do."

This man. I was going to murder him by squeezing him to death with my thighs if he didn't fuck me soon. "I do want this. I want you so badly, James, that I can't wait for you to see for yourself what you do to me. Please, I need you."

His breath shuddered, and finally, he pressed his mouth to my core. Faster than I could gasp, he devoured me. After all the prolonged foreplay, I'd assumed James would take his time with this too, drawing out the slow tease. Instead, he sucked hard on my clit, flicked it with his tongue, and tugged at it with his teeth.

I could have died right then, but he slid two fingers inside and curled them upwards until I was seeing stars, and galaxies, and maybe the whole universe. He knew exactly how to light up every single nerve ending in my body. I guess that's what hundreds of years of practice got you.

My hands twisted into his hair as I rode his hand and bucked against his mouth. The force of the suction spun me out toward another orgasm until it was just out of reach. "Oh yes. Oh. Please make me come."

James raised his head from between my legs and growled. "Not yet little flower. I want so much more from you before you come."

I pressed my head back against the pillows, biting my lip and breathing hard. His fingers continued to work me, and my knees started to shake. "Please, James. I-I need you. I need more."

I was so close, and yet so far. Until he did the last thing I expected and the one thing that pushed me into the second earth-shattering orgasm of the evening. He sunk his fangs into my throbbing pussy.

My back arched and every muscle in my body clenched, including my lungs, and maybe even my brain. My world exploded and continued to explode over and over and over until he pulled his fangs out and licked the sting, soothing my clit into releasing me from nirvana.

I dropped my hips back down to the bed, and maybe I blacked out for a minute? Holy shit. Like. Holy, holy, oh, no, not holy. Whatever that was, we were doing again. A lot.

James crawled back up and over me, cupped the back

of my head, and drew me into a deep kiss. His tongue worked in and out of my mouth just as his fingers and fangs did between my legs. Good God, my heart was truly going to give out. And what a way to go.

"I said you were going to come on my cock, and you are." He pulled me up, wrapped his hands around the backs of my thighs and lifted me up like I was as light as a feather plucked from a duck.

I squealed anyway and encircled his hips with my legs and his neck with my arms. All that did was bring his body closer to mine. He pressed me against the headboard and slid his hands under my ass, dropping me down until his cock was notched at my entrance.

I didn't even know men came this big. It was probably exhausting for him, carrying that monster around all day in his pants.

"Hold on tight, naughty vixen, because I'm going to fuck you until we're both seeing stars this time."

As rough as he was, he slid his cock into me slowly and gently, allowing me time to adjust to his size. I'd love to think I'd want him to slam home on one fast and hard thrust, but this was so much better. Our gazes locked and neither of us wavered as he pushed in inch by inch until he filled me completely.

He was so damn big, and it felt beyond anything I'd ever imagined to be so fully connected to him like this.

"Ready, love?"

I took several rapid breaths and squeezed my inner muscles around him. I stifled my giggle when his eyes rolled back in his head.

"I'll take that as a yes." His control was at its limits, just like mine, and there was no more teasing, no more waiting. James thrust into me fast and hard, growling my name over and over. "Rose, fuck, Rose. You're so fucking perfect."

I wanted to whisper, or even shout, dirty things to him too, but this must be what getting your brains fucked out feels like, because I had nothing. "Perfect."

That's the best I could come up with.

James didn't seem to notice my lack of sexy talk, or if he did, he didn't mind that I was completely failing at it. He kissed me again, this time with all the same force of need I felt. We were both so desperate our teeth clacked together, and I think I nicked the tip of my tongue on one of his fangs.

James's body tensed and he broke the kiss. The tiniest smear of red clung to one of his fangs. He swiped his tongue across it and his eyes went red, and then so dark there was no color. He pressed one hand against the wall next to my head like he was trying to control himself, and his hips jerked.

I didn't want him in control, I wanted him to lose his shit like I had. I met the thrust of his hips and he growled. His thrusts went from fast and hard to frantic. He pounded into me, hitting all the right places, literally rattling the wall with the headboard behind us.

"Come for me now, little flower of mine." His words came at me like a hypnotic suggestion. He lowered his mouth to my throat and scraped his fangs across my artery.

"Now, flower. Come now." He bit down and my body detonated with pleasure and pain, pain and pleasure.

Something new, deep inside of me, fluttered right along with my orgasm. For a brief moment, my soul lifted out of my body and touched an empty place inside of James. In the bliss of this intensely erotic moment, I found my soul mate.

"James, oh yes, James, James." My voice was more than a moan, his name was a passionate scream from the innermost part of my being.

Eventually, the world stopped spinning and I melted against James, satiated from this new connection and aching from the viciousness of the sex and the sheer size of him.

He laid my exhausted, limp body down and curled up beside me, smoothing my hair with his fingers. I wanted to purr at his touch, but I was too worn out, and my throat hurt a bit from all the screaming of his name.

Sorry, not sorry.

I slept like the dead. But I was more alive than ever before.

The London sky was painted with hues of pink and orange as dawn broke, casting a warm light through the sheer curtains. I stretched languidly. My body hummed with a newfound level of rightness with the world, and my mind buzzed with the knowledge that I was now part of something much greater than myself.

"James," I murmured, turning to face him, "I just want you to know that I may not know squat about your world, but I'm all in. I'm actually kind of excited to discover all the bits of the vampire world. Oh, are you going to turn me into a vampire?"

"No, love. A Soul's Serenity does get some, let's say,

supernatural perks like no more aging, and no disease. But turning someone into a vampire is a different thing entirely."

Ooh. Supernatural immortality-type perks. Cool.

"But sweet flower. Being my Serenity isn't all rainbows and candy floss. The danger to you has increased exponentially. I will do whatever it takes to keep us safe, to keep you from harm, and our bond alive. I'll do it. I'm ready to fight for us."

"Good." I grinned, feeling bolder than I'd ever been in my life. "So, what's our first move?"

I feel like it should have involved lessons in turning into a bat.

It did not.

JAMES

"Our first order of business is to stay off the radar. We need to be cautious and avoid drawing attention to ourselves."

I could think of something we could do while we were laying low.

She nodded sagely, but with her next question her voice wavered slightly, and that brought my mind right back out of the gutter I was reveling in.

"Why is this happening? Is it just because you're a vampire? Am I just collateral damage or a pawn to them?"

I took a deep breath. It was time to reveal more about the reality of the supernatural world I'd just pulled her into. I should have told her everything last night before we began the bond, but, like the selfish asshole I was, I couldn't wait to make her mine.

"You were a pawn to them, but those hunters wouldn't have killed you. Human life is sacred to them above all others. Especially mine and the people I serve. Vampires aren't the only ones they hunt."

"Hot damn. These guys were behind the witch hunts in the Middle Ages and stuff, weren't they?" Her mind was deliciously smart.

"Yes. But there are many other supernaturals. The Order has a special hard on for vampires and people like Mary O. and the Council of Princesses." The more I let her figure out on her own, the easier it would be for her to accept everything.

"I knew it. Those ladies aren't descended from the royals hanging in all those portraits all over the castle, they are those royals. Margaret is Princess Margaret?" Her eyes shined bright as she put more of the pieces together. Then her face went supernova into excitement, and she clapped her hands over her mouth. "Oh my... that blonde... that was fricking Princess Diana? Holy cow, holy cow, holy cow."

She danced around the room like this knowledge was too much to contain. She'd taken finding out that I was an immortal blood-sucking monster like it was no big deal, but the fact that Lady Diana Spencer hadn't burned up in a horrible car crash? No, that was too much. Ah, humans. Weirdly adorable.

"Yes. They're all immortals, demi-gods. They don't age or get sick, but they can be killed in ways similar to humans. They've been ruling Europe as the royal families for thousands of years. Vampires were sworn into service to protect them."

An old pact made by the First Vampire and upheld to this day.

"But what about her boys? What about Charles? Wait is Camilla—"

"The boys and Charles are all in on it, as was Queen Elizabeth and all the rest of the royal family." We didn't talk about Camilla.

"The Queen." Rose gasped. "I forgot about the Queen. She just died. Or, I mean, I guess she didn't. But if they're all immortals, why did she die? I'm so confused."

Elizabeth II had been a pain in everyone's arses. She simply didn't want to retire and refused to. We all knew why. "That's the natural progression. The Immortal Royals marry and have children just like humans. During their first debut into society, they age and behave just as a human would to keep the rest of the world in the dark. When they choose, they fake their deaths, and pass on their titles to their progeny."

"Have none of the members of any royal family actually died? They're all what, hanging out in the capitals of Europe somewhere, like, out partying or something? I don't suppose they dress in outfits from their time period." She suddenly clapped her hands, all excited. "Ooh, I hope I get to design for Queen Victoria. Now there was a powerful plus-size woman."

She wasn't far off. Henry the VIII was a notorious partier, and still couldn't stay in a monogamous relationship to this day. But not a soul ever recognized him in his modern-day bad boy cliche outfit of black jeans and a leather jacket. "No. As I said, they can be killed, and many have. They fight amongst themselves like any powerful family does. They also have enemies, like The Order. The VIA does our best to keep them alive, but we aren't always successful."

"But also, what the hell?" Rose paced back and forth in

front of me, and I could practically see her brain working overtime to process everything. "I will never watch a history documentary the same, ever again. This has so many implications in European politics and history."

This was a lot for her to take in, so it probably wasn't the right time to tell her about the Kennedys.

"Right." She waved her hand around and continued her pacing. I bet if I watched that reality telly show of hers, I'd see her do the same thing when she was thinking through her designs. "So, vampires are like these Immortal Royals' secret service agents. I got it."

There was much more to it than that. We had divisions that protected, but also that investigated both at home and abroad, and then there was the special ops unit I was a part of. But she didn't need all the details of the org chart. "Not all vampires. There are outcasts who have betrayed our kind, and I fear Gabriel could be... joining their ranks."

It was the only explanation I could come up with. We'd learned a vampire had betrayed us, and it had been too easy for The Order to kidnap Rose. Gabriel had been the one who suggested we let those hunters get away. He was the perfect distraction.

Rose's eyes widened, shock and confusion playing across her features. "Gabriel? But isn't he, like, in charge of your team?"

Yes. And my oldest friend.

"He is. If there's even a possibility he's turned dark, this endangers all the Immortal Royals and will tear the VIA apart." My chest tightened as I spoke, the thought of my closest friend betraying me too painful.

Rose dashed for the landline phone on the other side of the couch and starting dialing. "If Gabriel really is the traitor, and I'm not convinced about that, but if he is, Anna isn't safe."

Anna, her assistant? "In Chicago? I think she's fine."

"No. She's at the castle. She was there when I was taken. Slapped around pretty good by the bad guys too. I should have already called to tell her I'm not dead, but, you know, I was busy."

Rose dialed and I glared at the phone as it rang. When had Anna arrived and how? Why wasn't I either notified she was coming or been asked to escort her as well? Was this one more clue that Gabriel had taken over this mission and hung me and Rose out to dry?

When she finally picked up, Rose sighed out her relief, not yet making those same connections. She was simply worried for this woman who worked for her. "Hey Anna, are you all right? I can't believe everything that's happened. I called as soon as I could, to let you know I'm safe."

Thanks to my enhanced sense of hearing, I didn't need her to put the call on speaker to hear every word this assistant of hers was saying.

"Where are you?" Anna asked, her voice strangely not as worried for her boss as someone who witnessed them being kidnapped should be. "Are you even in Scotland?"

"Uh, no," Rose replied, and gave me a look that showed she was catching on to that tone same as I was. Good girl.

I put my fingers to my lips to indicate she should stay quiet about our location. She nodded and said, "I'm... somewhere safe, but I can't say where."

"Right, well, good you're not dead or something," Anna said, sounding completely uninterested in Rose's well-being, and like she was rushing her off the phone. "Anyway, don't worry about the dress for Mary O. I've got it under control. You don't need to come back to the castle."

"Wait, what?" Rose was totally surprised by Anna's dismissal. I was not. This was just another clue. "But my work—"

"Trust me, Rose. It's handled." Anna hung up before she could press for more information from her.

Rose stared at the phone for a full thirty seconds before she set its back in its cradle. "Well, that wasn't suspicious at all."

"Rose, I don't like this," I said, my unease growing as I paced the small room. "Anna's behavior is suspect. I didn't even know she was at the Black Castle when you were taken."

"I didn't know she was coming either. She just showed up right before I was... oh, oh no. Was she in on it?"

"Could she be involved with The Order of Vampire Hunters?" I mused aloud, my protective instincts on high alert.

"She seems so nice and competent. I'm having a hard time believing she's some crazy zealot like those guys at the restaurant."

"How well do you know her?"

"I only hired her a few weeks ago. She's been a godsend, helping me get my new line ready. She had references. But I suppose anything can be faked. I need to get a hold of Jorge and make sure he's all right." Rose's forehead creased with worry.

"Call him but be cautious. Just check in as if everything is going swimmingly here."

Rose chatted with her friend and did an excellent job not revealing any of her worries. He reported that Anna had said she had Covid and had called off work for the last few days. It made me wonder just how soon after I left with Rose that Anna had reported to her superiors and gotten on a plane too. But what was her end game?

I couldn't believe, even if she was working with Gabriel, that they'd simply assassinate Mary O. She had clout, but in the grand scheme of the Immortal Royals, she wasn't a major player. And if that was the plan, why take Rose, and leave Mary O. unharmed that morning?

Fuck. We needed to get back to the Black Castle, warn Mary O., or find someone who could. But I didn't have a clue who I could and couldn't trust anymore. It was too risky to trust anyone in the VIA. "I have to get back to Scotland, love. I can call in some favors and find a place to hide you, but I can't let whatever is about to happen go down without trying to stop it."

Rose put her hands on her hips in a pose reminiscent of Wonder Woman, and it was so damn sexy, I almost threw her over my shoulder and dragged her back to the bedroom. I knew what was coming and was already warring with myself over it.

I couldn't put her in danger. But she already was.

"You're not going anywhere without me."

Before I could even try to argue with her, there was a knock at the door. We both stilled and I motioned for her to hide. I'd spent my weapons in the fight at Franco's, but the kitchen was well equipped with steak knives. I slipped two into my belt and fisted another two while creeping toward the door.

"Vond. Open up."

Silvanus? Gabriel had brought him up to the Black Castle, so he could be in on this whole thing. If he was, I'd find out right now and kill him before he could report back. Cautiously, I opened the door, then yanked him inside, knife to his throat.

"How did you find us?" I demanded, letting the full ire of my monster out to play. Silvanus was young and hadn't fully developed his other forms, so I had the distinct advantage here.

"Relax, Vond. It wasn't hard. I tracked you to the restaurant and followed the reek of garlic here." He wasn't even the tiniest bit threatened, and his reply came with a confident grin. Either he was stupid or was actually on my side.

"Are you working for Gabriel?"

"Aren't we all?" That question had caught him off guard. That, plus the fact that his father had been so loyal as to give his life in service to the Immortal Royals was all the evidence I needed to see he had no clue what was really going on.

I released him but pointed one of the knives at his face. "Perhaps. Why are you here?"

He was silent for a moment, and I watched him closely as he processed what had just happened. It wouldn't be the last time another agent of the VIA threatened his life. He took it in fucking stride though. "I've got some important intel for you."

"Intel?" Rose poked her head around the corner, brandishing a fireplace poker in her hand. She'd also fashioned the bedsheet into a modest and functional toga-style dress, so Silvanus didn't get to see any of what was mine. What a woman. "What kind of intel?"

"A shipment of poisoned material, a list of targets," Silvanus pulled a folder from inside his jacket, "including Mary O.'s birthday party and the King's upcoming coronation."

"Alright, Silvanus," I said reluctantly. "Let's hear what you have to say."

"You're not going to like this next part, so, quite literally, do not kill the messenger. I just found the intel. Got it?"

I scowled at him. "No promises."

"There's also something in here," he tapped the folder, "about Rose being targeted because she was meant to be the mate of a vampire, even before you two met."

My vision went hazy red, and I had to grip the kitchen counter, so I didn't lash out and murder Silvanus just for standing there and delivering news. How could they have known about Rose's destiny to be mine?

ROSE

Silas filled us in on the details of his findings and I was flabbergasted by how super-secret, sneaky spy, deep state, double oh seven this whole thing was. Poisoned material? Assassination attempts? Moles in the very organization created to keep the royals safe? And then there was me. They'd known I was fated to be with a vampire before I even met James?

The Order had a whole frigging file on me. Like, from birth. So creepy.

"James," I whispered, needing his reassurance. I was absolutely shook by all these revelations. "We got this, right?"

He looked at me, his expression serious and determined. "We do. We protect those who need us, and we figure out who's behind all of this."

"Agreed," Silas chimed in. He had a cockiness about him that, if I wasn't already soul deep in love with James, I would find kind of sexy.

"Alright, then." I took a deep breath, pulling from that

same place I had when it was do or die on the Great Big Fashion Off. Sure, this was life or death for real, but let me tell you, sometimes it felt like that on the show. The inner strength I needed came from the same place inside either way. "Let's get to work."

Silas continued to describe the poisoned material, and my mind raced. The words he spoke sounded eerily familiar.

"Wait," I interrupted, my voice wavering. "Poisoned material? I thought you meant like some kind of powder or a substance. But you're talking about fabric, aren't you?"

"Yes, I think it says here it is called Luxury 3D Floral Multicolor Embroidery Flower Haute Couture lace." Silas read off a paper with a sales receipt photocopied to it. "I assume you know what that means."

Uh, yeah. "That's the fabric I ordered for Mary O.'s dress."

"Are you sure?" James asked, his expression darkening with worry.

"Positive." My chest tightened. "It's from a specialty shop right here in London called Bathory's. Anna recommended them."

"First Vampire be damned, they aren't very creative, are they?" James rolled his eyes. "Erzebet Bathory and her daughters were some of the most prolific vampire hunters of their time."

"Elizabeth Bathory? The Hungarian Countess... who ruled over part of Transylvania and was accused of torturing hundreds of people and possibly bathing in their blood, was a vampire hunter?" That actually made a lot more sense than she was just a crazy rich serial killer obsessed with her looks.

"She was. The Bathory's were humans granted access to the Immortal Royals way back in the thirteenth century by Vladislav IV. " James made a face of disgust. "They are a large part of why very few humans are allowed into our world. Their betrayal changed our world. Her descendants are card carrying members of The Order to this day."

"Dammit. The lady on the phone was so nice. I was going to try and visit them before I went back to America to chat about becoming a regular supplier for me." How long had they been planning this mission to have set up a whole website with reviews and everything? I never would have found them either, if Anna hadn't said they would be the best supplier of couture fabrics for this project.

Anna. Who'd quoted Lady Bathory in her interview.

"Uh, you don't happen to know what the Bathory daughters were called, do you? I have seen a show about her, but I could be misremembering." I did not like the connections all meshing together in my brain right now. "I have a horrible hunch."

"They are not women I am likely to ever forget. I was a young vampire when they had their reign of terror." He narrowed his eyes as he recited their names. "Katalin, Orsoyla, and the eldest, named for her grandmother, Anna."

As James said the final name, he looked at me and made that same connection I had. Anna, my assistant, wasn't in any danger. She was the danger.

"Alright." James's jaw clenched as he processed this added information. "We need to get back to Black Castle and warn Mary O. your assistant is a murdering zealot, and she definitely has plans for that dress."

Silas interrupted, clearing his throat. "Our duty is to protect the Immortal Royals. I'm sorry to be the one to point this out, but Rose will be a distraction if she goes back to the castle with us."

James didn't acknowledge Silas but stared at me with at least a dozen and a half emotions running through his eyes. His inner turmoil was evident, and I could see the weight of his responsibilities pulling him in opposite directions. My heart ached for both of us.

We'd just declared ourselves to each other, and we were already being tested. I had full faith in James, in us. Even if it had only been a few hours. He was who I was meant to be with. I knew this with my whole soul.

We'd figure out a solution or a compromise, but it could not be something that was going to get him killed while trying to do his job and keep me safe at the same time. I wouldn't have it.

I'd love to say I could take care of myself, but while I might have some new immortal perks, or at least I thought I did, I still couldn't turn into a bat, and I had few ninja skills that didn't involve either a sewing machine or a baguette. "I want to say we can face anything together, but that's just a cliche that could get us both killed. Should I just stay here?"

"No. If The Order knew about you before we met, you wouldn't be safe. Silvanus found us far too easily, they could too."

Silas shook his head. "To be fair, tracking is one of my extra sensory powers. You're sure we can't trust Gabriel? What about Fleming? Surely our local nerdy gadgets guy hasn't gone dark."

"If anything, F would be too easily manipulated by Gabriel." James shook his head and his eyes narrowed into a look I was coming to recognize as his thinking face. "Until we know for sure, one way or the other, we can't trust them. But if we're going to make this work, we need someone who absolutely wouldn't give two shits about The Order or their agenda. Someone who has experience guarding those in his care."

"The fact that every other agent on the Special Ops team is out on other assignments and not available does look like a point in Gabriel's become a bad guy column, doesn't it?" Silas drummed his fingers on the countertop. "I could use my father's contacts at VI6 to—"

"No, we need to keep this internal. If there's even a chance that I'm wrong about Gabriel, and I hope that I am, bringing in any other division would ruin all of our careers."

"It would be worth it to keep the Princesses and your Soul's Serenity safe." Silas looked between me and James.

"I appreciate that you're willing to make that sacrifice, kid. But I've got some contacts of my own, and some favors that it's time I call in," James said, his voice steady and resolute. "We can't face this alone, and I know just who to call."

"Ghostbusters?" I couldn't help it, the tension had to be broken just a little bit. "No, I know, you're friends with like, a supernatural Justice League?"

That did the trick, and James chuckled, but I could see the fire in his eyes. "Something like that. You're about to get a crash course in shifters."

Like shapeshifters? Fun.

"I need to make a few calls."

"Who are you calling?" I asked, feeling the familiar flutter of butterflies in my stomach as I wondered what new challenges awaited us.

"An old friend," he replied, pulling out his phone and dialing a number. "I trust him with my life."

The tension in the room thickened as we waited for the call to connect. Finally, a gruff voice answered, "Eyrik here."

"James," he replied nodding to me, reassuring me this was the help we needed. "We need your help. There's a plot against the Immortal Royals involving my Serenity and the Bathorys. We're headed to the Black Castle to stop it. We could use some backup."

"Fucking Bathorys," Eyrik replied, his voice serious and unwavering. "I'll gather the other former Volkov guards in the area and meet you there. It'll take us a few hours to get there from Prague. Your airstrip outside of Pitlochry safe to use?"

James confirmed the details to Eyrik and ended the call, returning his attention to me. "Eyrik is a wolf shifter who used to guard the Volkovs and the Wolf Tzar until their recent revolution. He's a trusted ally."

"A wolf shifter? Like werewolves? They had a Tzar?" Next, he was going to tell me that dragons were real too.

"Yes. Their new one lives in America though. Don't worry, love, they don't turn into slathering monsters during the full moon or anything," James reassured me, placing a gentle hand on my shoulder. "I've fought alongside Eyrik many times. We've saved each other's lives more than once."

"Okay," I breathed, trying to calm my nerves about meeting a real-life werewolf. "But I think you should also call in the Unicorn medic team."

"That's not a thing, sweet Rose," he said, his dark eyes softening as they met mine. "Although, unicorn blood is known to be all healing."

Duh. Everybody knew that.

"We're also going to need some weapons and supplies," Silas announced. "For both human hunters and vampires if you're right, Vond. We need to be ready for whatever comes our way."

"Might I recommend garlic pasta sauce?" I said it a bit jokingly, but also, that garlic really did seem to mess James right up when he'd come to rescue me.

"Got it," Silas said eagerly. "Let's go back to Franco's. They'll have plenty of weapons. And, at the very least, Rose here can make some garlic grenades.

"Garlic grenades?" I asked, raising an eyebrow in amusement.

Silas replied with a grin. "Trust me, they're your best tool when you're in a fight with vampire. We can't smell shit."

"He's right. The only reason I was able to find you in the midst of that garlic hellhole was because you're mine, mind, body, and soul."

I was and always would be. I couldn't help myself and gave him a quick kiss but slipped some tongue in there too. "No wonder you wanted to get me in the shower so quick after we got here."

"Ahem, can we save the kissy face for after we've foiled this plot to murder Mary O. and the Council of Princesses?"

"Yes, fine," I groused, as if I was put out. "Let's put an end to this poisonous scheme, so I can get back to jumping my sexy vampire lover's bones."

"Agreed," James replied, his eyes filled with the same need as mine.

"Do you two need some alone time before we go off and save the supernatural world?" Silas groaned.

"Yes." James and I said in unison.

Silas groaned.

"Just wait until you find your Serenity, newb. Don't worry, we'll make it quick." James threw me over his shoulder, and I didn't even protest because a girl could get used to being carried around when she knew she was about to have a really good orgasm.

I have Silas a little wave and a wink. "Be back soon. Maybe turn on the TV and turn up the volume?"

Approximately four minutes, three orgasms, and two freshly healing puncture marks on my throat later, and I had enough endorphins to take down The Order all by myself. "You have magic fangs and fingers, vampire of mine. Am I going to come every time you bite me?"

He grinned at me, all smug and satisfied with himself. "If I have anything to say about it, and I do, then yes."

"I'd say one more for the road, but we really should go save the world, I guess." I gave him a wink and a quick peck on the lips.

"It's only worth saving with you in it, sweet Rose." His expression was far from the playful banter of a few moments ago. He'd gotten all serious and heartbreakingly sincere on me.

"With all of my heart, I feel the same, so don't you even think about going and getting yourself staked in this battle. Or I will find a way to resurrect you and kill you myself for leaving me when things are just about to get good. You hear me?"

He grabbed my hand and kissed the inside of my wrist. "Together forever, Serenity."

Okay, just so we're clear. No one, except maybe Anna, was dying today. That was the plan, and we were sticking to it.

I rewrapped my toga dress and stole the shower slippers for shoes, then we headed out. James and Silas both stopped briefly at the front door and poured little vials of something over themselves. James gave his an extra shake and swore. "Damn. That's my last serum of sun."

Silas wiggled his little bottle and then shoved it in his pocket. "My last as well."

James sighed. "It'll last us the day, but we'd better hope this battle happens tonight, because come sunrise tomorrow, we'll fry without a resupply."

He stepped out into the sunlight, and I'll be damned, his skin sparkled. He was a sparkly fucking vampire. The effect only lasted for a moment, but he'd definitely sparkled like a teenage glitter bomb. "Huh. Any chance a certain author was allowed to do a VIA ride-along as research for her wildly popular YA series about vampires?"

"Of course not." James winked at me.

I peppered him with questions as we headed back to the scene of the crime. None of which he answered. I had a lifetime, or more than that now, to get it all out of him. I was so looking forward to life with him in this strange new world.

Just as soon as we saved it.

When we got back to Franco's, it was... fine. No broken tables and chairs, no dead bodies, no supernatural crime scene at all. There was a very stylish woman, about my size, brown hair perfectly coiffed, looking like she was straight out of a nineteen-sixties spy novel in her vintage Chanel 1959-60 Fall/Winter collection tweed suit, casually leaning against the doorframe.

"Ms. Primrose?" James gawked at her, and quickly went to her side with me and Silas in tow.

"James, Silas." She picked up a large, black duffle bag resting on the ground by her original Chanel slingback Cinderella slipper, two-toned high heels and dropped it at James's feet.

"You made quite a mess here, but it's all cleaned up. V sends his regards and good wishes for your," she slipped a look at me, and smiled, "mission. Don't let him down."

"Yes, miss." James's hand twitched like he really wanted to give her a salute.

Fascinating.

"Oh, and James? Watch out for Gabriel." Her expression didn't change from her business-like tone, but there was something behind her eyes that I recognized. She cared for Gabriel.

James's expression softened, but it was filled with real pain. "Eve. I—"

She didn't wait for his response. She sashayed away and melted into the other people on the street as if she'd never even been here.

"Who was that?" I also wanted to ask where she shopped because I want her entire wardrobe, but figured the whole mission thing was probably more pressing.

"Eve Primrose is V's secretary. Although that doesn't even begin to describe her position within the VIA. Nothing in any division happens without Ms. Primrose's say so. An order from her is the same as one from V."

Ooh. Girl power. I liked it. "I hope I get to, umm, have tea with her sometime."

"Let's make it through the night first, and then we'll see about introducing you to V. He's not known to have a fondness for mates or the vampires who find their Serenity."

Well, then he could kiss my plump ass. I wasn't going anywhere.

Silas zipped the bag open and found a whole cache of weapons inside. He pulled out a string of squishy white lumps, wrapped up in about eleven layers of cling wrap. "I think these are for you, Rose."

Garlic grenades. Sweet.

With our weapons and supplies in hand, we were ready to go. With every fiber of my being, I wanted to believe that we'd make it through this unscathed, but the reality was that nothing in this supernatural world was within my control.

"Ready?" I reached for James and traced the curve of

his jawline, marveling at the contrast between the rough stubble and the softness of his lips when he leaned into my touch.

"Guys, we need to get going," Silas called out, interrupting our moment. Reluctantly, we broke apart, knowing that the longer we delayed, the more danger Mary O. and the Immortal Royals would be in.

"Let's go," James said, his hand finding mine and giving it a reassuring squeeze.

My heart pounded with the weight of our decision. We had to return to Black Castle, not just for Mary O., but for all Immortal Royals who could be in danger. It was a gamble, one that put my life at risk, but it was the right thing to do. James wore a determined expression, his jaw set and his eyes focused.

"We need to make a quick stop." There was just one more thing I needed if we were going to go save the world. "When I talked to Jorge earlier, I asked him to post on my socials and find out from my followers where the best places to get cute plus size clothing were in London. I'm not rescuing an Immortal Princess in a bedsheet, no matter how well I styled it."

JAMES

The sun shined high in the sky as we set off toward Scotland. I could carry Rose in my bat form for a short distance, but not hundreds of kilometers, and not in direct sun. Where the fuck was Britain's infamous overcast weather when I needed it?

Ms. Primrose had, however, provided us with keys to a Mercedes lorry disguised as an ambulance, with a souped-up engine that easily exceeded the speed limit. That would cut our eight-hour drive down to four. Eyrik and his team would likely beat us to Pitlochry, but I trusted him to keep a low profile and possibly even scout for us while they waited.

As Rose rode in the seat beside me, her hand still firmly clasped in mine, I couldn't help but admire her resilience. She had been thrown into this world of danger and deception, yet she refused to back down or cower in fear. In her eyes, I saw the fire of determination, fueled by her love for me and our shared desire to protect those we cared for.

"James," Rose murmured softly, after we were out of the city and zipping up the M11. "I know my life isn't ever going to be normal after all of this. But are we going to always be constantly worrying about vampire hunters and immortal royalty? Like, do vampires get vacations or retire?"

"Sometimes," I admitted, allowing myself a brief moment to indulge in the fantasy of taking her to Iceland in the long dark winters to see the Aurora Borealis, or even exploring ancient ruins of history, many of which I'd seen being built in the first place hundreds of years before, but I'd see anew. I think she would like that. "But our love is anything but ordinary, why would our lives be? Perhaps that's what makes life with a fated mate extraordinary."

"Extraordinary," she echoed, a smile tugging at the corners of her lips. "I like the sound of that."

"Me too," I agreed, my heart swelling with affection for this incredible woman who had turned my world upside down. We were bound by something much stronger than fate, we were bound by love. And no force on Earth could break that connection.

Thanks to the drive, we arrived in Pitlochry near dusk, and I said good riddance to the setting sun that zapped my energy. If I was going to fight the hunters, I'd much prefer to do it in the darkest of nights when my powers prevailed, and their weak, fragile bodies were at a disadvantage.

I didn't want to think about having to battle Gabriel.

We parked the lorry near the rail station and headed toward the secret airfield on foot. It didn't take long for

Eyrik to find us. His wolf's eyes flashed in the partial moonlight from his hiding place in the trees. I looked around, ensuring there was no one else about, and he trotted over to us.

"Holy crap, that is one big ass wolf. I don't suppose I'm allowed to pet him, am I?"

Eyrik stuck his big old snout under Rose's hand, wagging his tail and making her giggle. I bared my fangs at him and hissed.

Rose laughed at me and withdrew her hand. She took a big step back when the cracking of bones and splitting of fur started. Eyrik shifted into his human form, and he was naked as a fucking jaybird.

"Oh." Rose covered her eyes and turned around. "Naked dude alert. Where are your clothes?"

Eyrik chuckled. "The Goddess's gift does not include clothes. That's the dragons you're thinking of. I won't be in this form for long, *sladkaya*. My wolf is much more powerful and dangerous."

"All the better to eat you with, my dear." Rose snorted at herself. "Wait, did you say dragons?"

She parted her fingers and stared up at me with a bit of frustration in those eyes. "Tell me someone has written some sort of guidebook for dating the supernatural beings in this world with an index for humans."

"I think I heard one of the Troikas' mates is a librarian and working on something like that." Eyrik winked at Rose, which I didn't have to kill him for because she still had her back to him and didn't see. I gave him a glower and he shifted back into his wolf form.

He gave a few short yips, and three more wolves came

trotting out of the trees. This was exactly the kind of back-up I'd hoped for. Neither Anna nor Gabriel would expect the wolves to come huffing and puffing at their door.

Silas and I put in our earpieces to communicate with. Ms. Primrose had stocked up our bag with weapons and basic comm devices, but there was only enough for the two of us. That was okay, I didn't want Rose to leave my side.

"Silas, team up with one of Eyrik's people and reconnoiter Mary O.'s location, and keep an eye out for Gabriel," I instructed the young vampire, who saluted with a smirk that reminded me of a rebellious teenager.

"King and country," Silvanus replied confidently before vanishing into the shadows with a large grey wolf.

"You two keep an eye out for the princesses as we get them evacuated." I pointed to the final two final wolves that had come with Eyrik, "and escort them down here to the airfield hangar. But keep an eye out for more hunters. Feel free to take them out if you come across any."

They yipped and trotted off toward the castle too. That left the three of us.

"Eyrik, you're with me and Rose." There were very few I trusted more than him. "Do not leave her side and protect her with every bit of strength and cunning you have. If I... if she and I are separated, keep her safe, and get her the fuck out of there."

He gave a little bark to acknowledge. Rose spun back around and gave him a quick pat on the head, which led to scratching him behind the ears until I hissed at him again. He just wagged his tail and let his tongue hang out the side of his mouth like he was fucking having fun.

"Alright, let's go find that poisoned fabric and the Bathory assassin."

Rose raised her hand. "Um, silly question. Where exactly is the castle?"

Oh shit. I pointed up the small hill to where the enormous stone structure shadowed the land. "What do you see there, love?"

She squinted, blinked, rubbed her eyes, and squinted again. "That's so weird. If I squint exactly right, I see it. But just looking in that direction, all I see are ruins."

Damn. "The castle has a spell on it so that nosy humans can't enter. To most, it does appear as dilapidated ruins. The charm I put on you must be wearing off."

"Okay, crazy. Squinting it is for me then." She shrugged and narrowed her eyes.

"I don't like this, but I don't have another charm. We'll try to get to Fleming's lab in the dungeon. He'll have a whole stack of them there that I would have been replacing daily if we'd been here at the castle." The only other alternative was to leave her here, and I wasn't comfortable doing that. "Just keep within arm's reach of either me or Eyrik, and we'll guide you."

"I can do this. I can." She straightened her spine and put a hand on my arm.

"I know you can." I had to believe in her. Rose was a smart and savvy woman who'd kicked butt and taken names a couple of times already since entering my world. I couldn't help but admire her determination. Despite all she'd been through, she never wavered. "Everything is going to be fine."

It was not. But we didn't have an alternative.

The castle was too quiet, and that already had me on edge. Mary was a notorious night owl, and I didn't hear a peep out of any wing. I clicked the comm link. "Silas, sitrep."

"No sign of anyone. Main living quarters clear. Headed to the dungeon."

This was not good. We made our way through the dimly lit corridors of the castle and up the stairs. At least I already knew this area was clear.

"Is this the room?" she asked, stopping before the ornate door to Mary's sitting room. She touched the wood, trying to feel her way. "I think it is."

I nodded. "This is where you met with Mary and the other princesses. Are your dressmaking supplies in here? Is this where the fabric would be?"

She pushed the door open, and we entered the sewing room, the faint scent of chamomile lingering in the air. Moonlight streamed in through the large window, casting eerie shadows on the walls.

I watched her navigate the room with ease, her fingers digging through the various gowns and fabrics.

Our search for the poisoned fabric was interrupted by an angry voice echoing through the corridors, shattering the quiet atmosphere of the Black Castle.

"James!" Gabriel's voice roared from the main entrance's grand hallway.

"Stay here, find the fabric." I commanded Rose and Eyrik, knowing neither would probably do as I said. I used my super speed and ran out to the stairway and jumped over the side to land right in front of the vampire formerly known as my best friend.

His golden eyes blazed with a fire in them, fury in every step as he stormed toward me. "I thought I could trust you, of all vampires, James. Now look what you've done."

I froze, my heart clenched with pain at the sight of my best friend's betrayal. How could I not have seen him sliding into the dark side and becoming the villain in his own twisted tale?

"Gabriel, listen to me." I crouched, ready to spring at his attack. "There's more going on here than you realize. There's a Bathory assassin here, and they're trying to kill Mary O. and the princesses."

"Save your lies," Gabriel snarled, his fists clenched at his sides. "You've done nothing but create distractions, pulling our attention away from Mary O. and her party. You're the real threat, Vond."

"Gabriel," my voice dropped an octave as the monster in me took offense, the weight of his accusations dragging me down. "I would never betray the Agency, my King, my country, or you."

"Prove it," he challenged, his gaze unwavering.

"Alright then." I took a deep breath, readying myself for the confrontation that was about to unfold. "Let's settle this like vampires."

The air between us crackled with tension as we circled one another, each waiting for the other to make the first move. It wasn't long before Gabriel lunged at me, his fangs bared and his supernatural strength on full display.

"Is this what you wanted?" He rammed into me, hurling me across the room with a single swipe of his arm. "To see vampires turn against one another? I had to tie Fleming up because he kept defending what you were doing."

"Never." I picked myself up from the wreckage of a toppled stone wall. "But I can't let you stand in our way."

With a guttural roar, I unleashed my own vampire powers, the ones I kept hidden deep inside, the ones too dark for anyone to ever suffer. The shadows around us bent to my will. I hurled a wave of darkness at Gabriel, forcing him back against the wall.

"I know you're the traitor, old friend," I growled, my voice laced with bitterness.

"James," Rose cried out, her eyes wide with fear as she watched our battle play out. "You don't have to do this."

"Stay out of this, Rose," I warned, never taking my eyes off Gabriel. "It's time I prove myself once and for all."

"Or perhaps," a quiet voice whispered in my ear, "you're simply trying to prove something to yourself."

"Enough," I snapped, casting one final shadowy attack towards Gabriel, who countered with an explosion of fog that sent me sprawling to the ground.

"Rose, I need you to listen to me," I said, my voice low and urgent. "I can't risk your safety. Get out of here and find that fabric. I'll handle Gabriel."

"James, no. You said..." Eyrik understood the task and shoved Rose back toward the sewing room. He'd keep her safe until I could end this.

"V was right to mistrust a fated vampire. She's manipulated you and made you weak, Vond." Gabriel's fog swirled around me. He poked and pushed at me, hidden within his vampiric powers.

If he was going to play dirty, so was I. "Ah, just as Eve has for you old man. Too bad you'll never have her."

That's when the world around me erupted into death and despair unlike the world had ever known.

ROSE

My heart raced as I slipped through the shadows, hands grasping Eyrik's fur, so I didn't miss a step and fall down and kill myself. I did as James asked, and we were headed back to the sewing room. But I wasn't going to just crouch in there and cry. No. I was going to get the evidence we needed to prove to Gabriel that James and I weren't traitors.

Of course, this plan only worked if Gabriel also wasn't a traitor. But I'd seen the way Eve had said his name and asked James to watch out for him. She hadn't meant watch out like be careful, she'd wanted us to care of him and make sure he was safe.

That was not the request of a woman who thought her man, umm vampire, had betrayed everything they fought for.

I pushed open the door and froze when Eyrik growled so deep and low I felt the rumble in my chest. There, standing in front of me, was a mirror image of myself. It was uncanny. She was the same height, had the same curves, even the same hairstyle. But there was something off about her expression, a wicked gleam in her eyes that sent shivers down my spine. I knew immediately that this was Anna, the Bathory assassin.

"Tell your wolf to back down, or I'll bring out the silver bullets."

Eyrik snarled and gnashed his teeth, putting himself between me and Anna. I could barely see over the top of him. "I think that's a myth, dummy. He's a wolf shifter, not a werewolf like in the movies."

"Shall we test that theory?" Anna did indeed bring out a very old-fashioned looking gun. But she didn't point it at Eyrik. Instead, she aimed for a figure in the shadows.

I squinted, and dammit all to hell. Mary O. was there, tied to a chair. From what James had explained, Mary could definitely be killed by a gunshot. But I had more intel on Anna and The Order's plans than she knew. "You won't kill her. If you do, she won't be able to wear the poisoned dress and kill all the rest of the Immortal Royalty coming to the party. Good try, Anna, but I've got your number. So just hand over the gun and come quietly."

That was a line straight out of some British crime show I'd seen on Netflix or somewhere. Sounded good. Didn't work in the show either though.

"Ah, so you finally figured it out," Anna purred, a malicious grin spreading across her face. "What gave it away? My impeccable taste in fashion?"

"Your taste in murder is more like it," I retorted, gritting my teeth. "You won't get away with this. The VIA have got you surrounded."

"Please, call me Rose," she mocked, her laughter cold and hollow.

"You only wish you could be me. I've got more than you can ever dream."

"Oh, your precious fated mate? You think James is going to save you? He's the patsy for this whole thing," Anna sneered. "You honestly believe that a vampire could ever love you? You're nothing but an abomination—a pathetic, desperate human clinging to the hope that you'll somehow be worthy of a creature like him."

"Shut. The fuck. Up." I kept my voice calm, but filled with all the venom I felt for this woman who'd ingratiated herself into my life and then stabbed me in the back. Almost literally. "You may have a whole ass file on me, but you don't know anything about me."

"Oh, but I do," she purred, stepping closer. "I've been watching you, studying you. I know your deepest fears, your darkest secrets. And I know that deep down, you're just like me—hungry for power, desperate for love. That's why I chose you, Rose. Because I knew that you'd make the perfect pawn in my little game."

Sounds like she was projecting. I could work with that.

"Your game?" I asked, my hands clenching into fists. Where was a baguette or a plate of spaghetti when ya needed one.

"Killing the Immortal Princess Mary of Orange and every last guest at her event." Her eyes gleamed with malice. "With them out of the way, there will be no one left to stop me from taking control of the supernatural world."

Oh, right. That game.

I was done playing. A dead Bathory assassin was almost as good as proof to show Gabriel as a live one. I hoped.

"I have a game of my own, it's called fetch." I released the fur on Eyrik's back that I'd been holding so tight. "Get her, boy, I mean big, scary wolf man."

Eyrik attacked and I sprinted for Mary. The ridiculously loud sound of gunshots reverberated off the stone walls, and I sure as shit hoped wolf-shifters really weren't killed by silver bullets. The wolf did give a little yelp, but it was covered up by Anna's screams.

Good. I hope he shook her to bits like a dog toy.

I literally skidded to stop myself from grabbing Mary straight up out of the chair. She wasn't even tied to it, but she was wearing the most godawful floral print dress I'd ever seen in my life. I did not design that shit. It looked like it was made for one of those Americana dolls, but by someone's grandma instead of from the store.

Yikes. This was the poison dress.

Couture handmade fabric, my ass.

"Mary, are you alive?" I looked around for a set of cutting shears so I could shred this piece of trash right off her.

Her head lolled, but she moved it from one side to the other. "Hurts."

Yes. I did the tiniest of fist pump celebrations. She wasn't dead. "Okay, hold really still. I'm going to get you out of this."

The dress wasn't finished, and if I hit just the right seams, the whole thing would fall right off her. I grabbed another bit of fabric nearby that looked nothing like this floral monstrosity, so I was hoping it was safe enough to cover my own hands with while I touched Mary and the poisonous dress.

The shears were oh, so sharp, and in just a few snips, the whole thing fell onto the chair and the floor beside her. I gathered some of it up as proof and wrapped it in the safety material.

But now Mary was in her small lacy things, and I had to guess they had residual poison on them as well. They were going to have to go too. Sad, because they were super pretty and probably mega expensive. Plus, there was no way I was dragging a royal princess around a castle bare-ass naked. She wasn't a wolf shifter who was used to that kind of thing. Probably. What did I know?

That I wouldn't want to be dragged around a castle in my birthday suit. The muslin I'd been laying out for Mary's dress approximately four billion years ago, before I'd been kidnapped, was still on the dress form. It was only partially pieced together, but that would just make it easier to get on her.

I grabbed it off the form and yanked it over her head. Then I snipped her bra straps and band, so it fell off, and did the same to the sides of her panties. "Sorry, sorry. Just trying to make sure you don't die."

"But I want her dead." Anna's hoarse, broken voice came from behind me, and she yanked me back.

I stumbled, but managed to stay upright, scissors in hand. "You're going to have to go through me."

That was a really strange thing to say out loud to someone who literally looked just like me. But it was really just to buy some time. Because behind Anna, Eyrik was getting up off the floor. He had blood all over him and was still bleeding out of what looked like bullet wounds in his chest, shoulders, and face. But even in the few seconds that I watched him, I could see the wounds healing right before my eyes.

In a desperate bid to give Eyrik a head start on attacking and, hopefully this time, killing Anna, I first flung the scissors at her, haphazardly. Then I hurled a nearby sewing machine at her, the heavy object connecting with her head and sending her stumbling backward. Ooh. Was this one of my new immortal perks, super strength? Fun.

Seizing the opportunity, I grabbed Mary by her floppy arm and dragged her from the room, my heart pounding in my chest as we raced down the shadowy corridors that I could barely make out. Please don't let me fall down the stairs and break my neck.

As we neared the main entryway, the sound of a fricking video game style fight, with enormous crashes that sounded like whole buildings fell down around us, reached my ears. Skidding to a halt, I peered around the corner, squinted hard, and saw James still locked in a heated battle with Gabriel, both of them snarling and baring their fangs. It seemed that whatever fears the two of them had about each other had come to a boiling point.

"Gabriel," James roared, "Get your head out of your arse and listen to me," James insisted, his eyes blazing with that scary blood red. "There is a Bathory assassin here in the castle, right now, and we need to stop her before it's too late."

"Why should I believe anything you have to say?"

Gabriel spat, his handsome face contorted with rage. "It's clear where your loyalties lie—not with the Vampire Intelligence Agency or our mission, but with your human lover."

"Enough!" I cried, stepping into the room and interrupting their argument. The two vampires whirled toward me, surprise flashing across their faces. "I have proof of the assassin's identity and her gruesome intentions."

James looked at me with concern. "Rose, are you alright? Where's Eyrik? What happened?"

"Words later, proof now," I said, yanking Mary's dress down to cover her up, and then pulling her out from the shadows.

Her head lolled, but she was standing, so... I slapped her. I slapped a princess. Whichever gods she was descended from, forgive me. "Tell them what just happened."

"Doppleschmanger," Mary slurred.

"There," I said, thrusting Mary O. toward Gabriel, who, luckily, did his duty and caught her before she fell at his feet. "Anna, my so-called assistant, she's the assassin. She tried to manipulate me into being part of her twisted plot. I think Eyrik might be eating her face off right now, or you could see that she clearly used some kind of magic spell or something to look like me."

I held the sack of material out and shook it around. "She made this fugly dress for Mary and look what it did to her."

Gabriel stared at Mary for a moment, then at the material I held aloft, his expression unreadable. Then, slowly, he lifted his gaze to meet James's. "Fuck. James. I was wrong to doubt your loyalty. This never should have happened on my watch."

"Apology accepted," James replied, his voice strained but sincere. "Now, let's figure out how to stop this maniac before she kills everyone at the event."

My heart swelled with relief that they were both on the same side now.

"Oh, I'm pretty sure she's dog food right now."

Both men looked at me like that was the grossest thing anyone had ever said to them. "What?"

Gabriel gave me a smirk that might have melted the panties off a lesser woman. Not that I thought Ms. Eve Primrose was lesser than me. I did wonder if she'd had her panties melted off though. "You've integrated far too easily into our world, Ms. Abernathy."

"Why thank you, Mr. uh..."

"Just Gabriel."

"We don't know that Anna is the only member of The Order here," James interjected, bringing us back on task, "and I haven't been able to get a sitrep from Silvanus since we entered the castle."

"I had Fleming put up jammers when I thought you'd gone rogue."

"Was that before or after you tied him up?" James poked at Gabriel.

It was probably going to be a while before these two trusted each other fully again. I clapped my hands, putting on my bossy boots voice, "Time is of the essence, boys. Let's get everyone out of here."

"Agreed," James replied, his strategic mind already at

work. "Let's get Fleming first, so he can get comms back up and running. Then we'll evacuate the ladies and their staff."

"They're all down in the dungeon. I thought it the safest place to contain everyone."

"Ooh. I bet those princesses did not like being locked in the dungeon," I sing-songed like Gabriel was in trouble.

He shrugged. "Not the first time for several of them. They're fine."

"Everyone, you must leave immediately," Gabriel bellowed as we entered the room, his authoritative voice cutting through the chatter like a knife. Or rather, the giggles.

All the princesses were in a clump, surrounding someone who was getting all of their attention.

"What's going on?" I asked.

The princesses parted, and we found Fleming, still tied to his chair, in the center of the circle of women, his magnifying glasses askew, the top few buttons of his shirt unbuttoned, and covered in lipstick kisses. He had quite the goofy grin on his face too.

"Just having a little fun to pass the time while mean old Gabriel had us locked in the dungeon," Margaret said, and snapped the top back on a tube of lipstick.

I almost hated to interrupt. "We just thwarted an assassination attempt on Princess Mary O.," I explained, keeping my own giggles in. This was serious business. "We need to get her to a, um, supernatural doctor? And evacuate the rest of you until we know it's safe."

The ladies all gathered themselves up and began filing out of the room single file like recalcitrant schoolgirls.

"Head out the back door, ladies, and you'll find some wolf-shifters waiting to escort you to the airfield," I continued to direct them.

"Oh, yay, puppies," one of the princesses clapped her hands and hurried the rest of them along.

Gabriel leaned over to James and stage whispered so that I heard him perfectly well. "Who put her in charge?"

James chuckled and said, "I'm not sure, but I think it might have been V."

JAMES

We sent Silas and the wolves off to get the princesses all packed up and safely on their way to their various castles around the country, while Gabriel and I gathered up all the intel for our after-action report and debrief. We needed to get our shit together fast, because Prim was on her way. Ostensibly to collect Mary O. and take her to be treated. Fleming was already working to analyze the poison.

He'd been muttering all morning about this compound and that spell. Rose leaned over and whispered in my ear. "I think his brain is a little on overdrive after all that, uh, affection, from the princesses."

Fleming wasn't exactly the suave gentleman vampire, nor the alpha protector type. But he had something about him that the ladies loved.

Gabriel rubbed his hands together. "Let's piece together what the hell happened here, shall we?" He did like a puzzle. "Starting with our dead assassin upstairs and working our way backwards."

"Anna was the lynchpin member of The Order to execute this mission." Had it not been for my amazing mate, we may never have detected this kind of subterfuge. "But she had to have help beyond the lackies we've encountered. This was a much more sophisticated plan than their usual slash and kill routine."

Usually, the Order just came at us head on. We'd have to start adjusting the way we dealt with them, because they were clearly evolving to have a much more sophisticated strategy. The dumbass zealots at the restaurant were the kind I was used to dealing with. Sure, they could be deadly, but they were simple. Kill the vampire, or witch, or wolf, or immortal, because they weren't human. The end.

Anna's plan had been that, but with so much more nuance than kill or be killed.

"Yes," Gabriel nodded. "I suspected The Order had some new blood. For them to have laid a trap that pitted us against each other as a distraction is brand new territory."

Rose raised her hand in an adorable school-girl kind of way. I'm not sure why, she'd basically taken over this mission and was practically an honorary member of the VIA's Black Ops at this point. "I thought The Order was just humans. But Anna used some crazy doppelganger magic spell, clearly had one of these charm thingies that let her find the castle, and was attacked by the biggest werewolf, sorry wolf-shifter on the planet, and managed to survive a long time while he was tearing her to shreds. So, what gives?"

Good point.

Fleming poked his head in. "Yes, I'd like to examine the assassin's body to determine if she was simply using stolen magic, and, if so, what kind, or if she's been somehow enhanced."

"God dammit, I hate it when they twist their own rules."

Rose's eyes went wide. "Can you even say that? The G-word?"

I grinned at her and pulled her into my arms. "Only when he's really mad."

"Quite right. I am angry. This went down on my watch." Gabriel pointed at me and F. "Vond, go get the assassin's body. Fleming, I want you to examine every cell and figure out exactly what we're dealing with."

"Ooh, autopsy," Rose said. "Also, eww. No thank you, I'll skip that part, thanks. I've had enough blood and guts for one day, thank you very much."

I pulled her into my arms and kissed the top of her head. "We'll finish up here and then get you into a nice hot shower, okay?"

Rose waggled her eyebrows at me. "Yes, please. Showers are my favorite. I may never take a bath ever again."

"I'll be right back." I headed up the stairs, grateful for a minute of quiet to think. Gabriel and Fleming could finish preparing the report. I, too, was looking forward to a shower. I may not need sleep, but the last few days had depleted my energy.

If it hadn't been for Rose's blood giving me the sustenance only she could provide, I might be in literal pieces right now, taken down by The Order.

But after we filed our paperwork and debriefed, and this mission was completed, I needed to have a meeting with V about my future with the VIA. I loved this work, but I loved Rose more.

We'd bonded, but I hadn't yet asked her to share her soul with me and become my true Serenity. I still wanted it to be her choice. My need shouldn't dictate her life.

We could go on for years being lovers. I could take her blood and give her the world and a whole lot of orgasms in return, but she would age, and live a mostly normal life, her soul intact. When she died, I would too, eventually.

We simply hadn't had time for me to explain all of this to her. I told myself she would be in less danger if I didn't. She'd already been targeted though, so my logic was off.

Later. Once she'd rested, I would tell her everything. I would pull my head out of my ass and ask her to share her soul with me so that we could be together forever.

On my way up, I noted the shit ton of damage Gabriel and I had done to this castle. Sunlight streamed in through the broken walls, and there was a lot of repair work to be done to make the Black Castle safe again. I'd grab some more serum of sun from F when I brought him the body.

I entered Mary O.'s sitting room, surprised by how much damage had been done here too. Eyrik had really torn the place up. One more thing to add to the to-do list.

Anna's body was in a shadowed corner of the room, so I skirted the edge of the sunlight, not wanting to waste my energy on healing from burns. I squatted next to the body, that had now reverted to her natural state. Thank goodness she didn't still look like Rose. That would have creeped me the fuck out.

Anna's eyes popped open and glowed a deep, vampiric red.

"Ah, James," she purred, fangs glinting as she smiled wickedly. "I was wondering when you'd show up."

First Vampire be damned, Anna had been turned, and she wasn't fucking dead. I snatched her by the throat and pinned her to the floor.

"Your plan failed, Anna," I declared, my voice steady despite the adrenaline coursing through my veins. "You've given up your beliefs and your soul in this battle. Why?"

She writhed against me, the strength of a newly turned vampire on her side. "I will sacrifice everything to destroy you. You're monsters that need to be sent back to hell."

"Bold words for someone who'll be joining us there." I reached for a broken table and cracked off one of the legs to use as a stake.

Her second life as a vampire may have just begun, but I was going to end it now. I drove the stake into her chest and twisted it for good measure.

She shuddered in her death throes, but her screams turned to laughs.

What. The. Actual. Fuck?

Anna lunged at me with preternatural speed and strength. Holy hell. She shouldn't be able to move like this. She shouldn't even be alive.

I dodged her attack, parrying her first blows, but we danced around the room, both trying for any advantage. There was no avoiding the rays of sunshine pouring in through the open gashes in the walls, and they were only getting wider and brighter as the sun rose higher in the sky.

With her next attack, I shoved Anna directly into one of the shafts of light. She screamed for real this time and her skin sizzled in the heat, acrid smoke wafting off her burns. New vampires were entirely more susceptible to the light of day.

That was my advantage, but it also meant I could not use my power over darkness in this battle at all.

She screeched and literally climbed the nearest wall and up to the ceiling like a fucking spider. "History will remember me as the one who brought down an empire!" she snarled, her eyes wild with madness.

"No," I countered, jumping up to meet her, my fists connecting with her jaw in a satisfying crunch. "History won't even know your name. You'll go into a report in a dusty file in the basement at Chattering as a failed assassin, and nothing more."

"James!" Rose's voice called out just as I delivered a blow, sending Anna crashing into the door. The impact shook the room, dust raining down from the ceiling like ash. The entire west wall collapsed on top of Anna and sunlight streamed in.

"Rose, stay back." I warned as I surveyed the damage. There was no path to her that wasn't bright with the burning light of the sun, and I couldn't be sure if Anna was trapped or dead under the truckload of stone she was buried beneath.

The pile of rubble moved, and Anna hissed from within. One arm reached out and grabbed Rose, even as her flesh lit on fire.

Rose thrashed and writhed against Anna's grasp, but she was stronger now than when Eyrik had taken her down. "Die, you stupid zombie-ass bitch, die."

I summoned every ounce of strength and will-power I had left to finish this once and for all. No one hurt my Rose and lived to tell about it. Anna was going down, even if it meant I had to sacrifice everything to drag her to hell with me.

With a roar, I jumped into the light and dashed toward Rose and Anna.

"James, what are you doing?" Rose's voice echoed in my mind even through the intense pain of the sun burning me alive. I could feel her fear for me, but I pushed it aside. This was the only way to ensure her safety, and the safety of everyone else.

"I have to finish this." I gritted my teeth against the pain that threatened to consume me. "I love you, Rose. Remember that."

"James, no!" she screamed at me, but there was no turning back now.

Bracing myself, I used the last of my strength and leapt into the air, crashing into Anna, and out through the hole in the side of the castle. We crashed onto the green, grassy garden below, the sun full and bright.

Anna immediately burst into an eruption of flames and turned to ashes, even as she still reached to claw at my face.

As I slipped into unconsciousness, I clung to the vision of my gorgeous Rose and the knowledge that I had done everything I could to protect the one I loved.

I floated in the abyss, waiting for hell to consume me.

At least I hadn't asked Rose to share her soul with me, sealing her fate in this hell as well.

"Wait a minute. Who is this douchepotato? He is not one of ours. What's he doing in our afterlife, my love?" A male voice with the power of a thousand alphas behind it resonated through my mind.

I blinked and found myself not in the darkness of hell but surrounded by pure white light. And, was that a rainbow? A rainbow dragon?

Why the fuck was he here? I tried to speak, to ask where I was, but nothing came out.

"No, no, love of my life. I think he's just passing through. Look at how brightly his Serenity's soul shines for him. He won't be here long. Probably just learning an important life lesson about not screwing around, being scared of claiming the real love in his life when it's offered to him." A woman with a lush voluptuous body and dark olive-brown skin highlighted by her white flowing gown waved at me and winked.

"Oh yes, heart of mine, I see it now. Go on, kid. Oh, before you go, let me give you a piece of advice. Lots and lots of orgasms. Mates like that." The dragon flew in circles around and around me, making me dizzy.

First Vampire save me from these fucking dragons.

ROSE

*E*very beat of my heart felt like it would be the last. My chest and throat burned like I was the one on fire. I fell to my knees at the edge of the precipice of rocks that used to be the side of the Black Castle, squinting to hold back the sun and my tears.

Gabriel and Fleming rushed into what was left of the room, both ready to fight, both too late. I pointed to the lawn outside, gasping for air between sobs. "Please. Help. Me. Save. Him."

He couldn't really be dead. He couldn't.

"Rose, we haven't got a moment to lose." Gabriel's voice cut through the dimly lit room as he urgently grabbed me, preparing to jump down into the light. "There's a chance, but James needs you."

Fleming pulled a cannister from somewhere inside his jacket and sprayed Gabriel down with the glittery serum. Then he shoved it into my hands. "Cover him in this first, it will stop the effects of the sun from doing more damage while you work."

I nodded and took the spray. Then I turned to Gabriel and let him wrap me in his arms. I thought we'd jump down, but in a weird whoosh of cold wet air, my world went all foggy, and poof, we reappeared in the grass.

Gabriel kicked the pile of ashes that used to be Anna away, and I squirted the serum across James's body as fast as I could. The flames on his skin and clothing went out, but he lay as still as a corpse.

"Is it enough, will he be okay?" I couldn't help the tremor in my voice. I was still grappling with the fact that Anna had turned herself into a vampire even after she knew she wasn't going to be able to carry out her plans, just so she could kill me and James.

I wasn't ready to deal with the part where James, my fated mate, sacrificed himself to save me.

Gabriel lifted James's still form and carried him into the nearest standing structure, what looked to be a gardener's shed, to get him out of the sunlight. He set him back down on the ground in the cool shade of the room, but shook his head, looking terrifyingly defeated.

"Listen, Rose. The only reason he didn't burn up like Anna is the strength he's gained with age, but he's floating between life and death right now. Only you can save him."

"Me? How? I'll do anything. Does he need my blood? Take it, take it all." I held out my wrist and, when Gabriel didn't move, searched for something I could use to cut my own veins open.

Gabriel clasped my arm and held me still. "Yes, your blood, but he won't need much, not if you can share your soul with him." Gabriel's expression softened for a moment. "He should get to ask you this yourself, and I'm sure he would have. It's his only hope."

Share my soul? "It's his. I swear it."

"It takes more than words, but beyond that, only those who've done it understand how. The bond is formed when you have a deep emotional connection."

Didn't we already? I'd accepted James for everything that he was, and he'd done the same for me. "Are there words I have to say or something? I don't know what to do. What if I can't do what he needs?"

I didn't know what to do.

I didn't know how to be what he needed.

My heart hammered against my sternum, feeling as if everything inside was going to break from the pounding.

"Gabriel, I..." The hesitation cracked my voice, betraying my fear, but also my desire to do anything for James. Ms. Primrose appeared in the doorway and pushed her way into the shed, took in the situation, and grabbed Gabriel by the arm, as if needing his strength. I looked at them both, pleading for them to tell me what to do.

This wasn't a sewing challenge, some business opportunity, a reality tv show game. This was life and death, and not something I could win just by being focused and giving it my all. I'd taken on haters, trolls, judges, and the public that were all fatphobic, and created my own little empire from living my life as big and as loud as I could.

None of that was going to help me save James.

I'd fought off vampire hunters, thrown a sewing machine at an assassin, made friends with a wolf, and loved a vampire.

I didn't know how to be anything more than what I

was. I was always too much for the rest of the world, and I thought in James, I'd finally found someone I was just the right amount for.

"What if I'm not enough?"

Ms. Primrose kicked off her Chanel heels, peeled off her jacket, handing it to Gabriel, and knelt down beside me. "Fate chose you for a reason, Rose. You're the only one who is the exact right kind of special for him. Your love for James is something that can't be denied, nor his for you."

She was right. Despite the doubts and uncertainties that plagued me, I knew that I would do whatever it took to save the man I loved—the vampire who had shown me what it truly meant to be alive.

"Alright," I whispered softly, my breath catching in my throat as I decided what to do. "I'm going to try something, and if vampires, and whatever you are Ms. Primrose, have every prayed, now would be the time."

I had to shake off the lingering fear and uncertainty that clung to me. But beneath it all, I could feel the fire of determination and love beginning to burn brighter, fueled by my desire to save the man who had captured my heart.

Another vampire entered the shed, and his presence filled the room like a thick fog. He looked down at me and then at James. "Your bond is a force to be reckoned with. You two are unstoppable together. It's why I sent for you."

"Unstoppable," I repeated, letting the word wrap around me like a weighted blanket, providing warmth and comfort. I didn't know who this dude was, but I liked him, and we were going to be friends, after I saved James.

"Exactly. Let that fire, the passion that ignites when

you're near him, guide you through this process." He draped the deep red cloak he was wearing around my shoulders and patted my hand.

"Okay." My breath hitched as I drew in a fortifying gulp of air, each molecule sparking the embers of courage within me. "Let's do this."

"James." I leaned in to whisper to him, my voice filled with equal parts desperation and resolve. "Hold on. I'm here… and I won't let you go."

"Alright, Rose," the vampire's voice was the whisper of wind through the trees, "you're ready. Remember, your love is the key."

"Love," I murmured, my heart pounding like the staccato beats of a metronome. "I can do this."

My hands trembled as I cradled James's face, feeling the chill of his porcelain skin beneath my fingertips. I remembered he'd made me feel protected and cherished in a world where I often felt like I had to prove myself. Now, shivering against the stark cold of his lifeless form, I knew I needed to summon that same feeling of safety from within me, to breathe it back into him.

"James," I whispered, my voice no longer trembling. "I want to dance beneath the moonlight with you, our laughter mingling with the rustling of the wind through the trees. I want to spend hours lost in the pages of our favorite historical biographies, debating the merits of kings and queens that I've only read about, and you keep safe to this day."

I felt something in my chest flutter like a candle struggling to stay alight. My soul reached out for his, but found only a deep dark empty place inside of him.

But that couldn't be right, James was the best of us all. He never wavered, he always did what was right. If that wasn't what a pure soul was, then none of us had one.

"Stay with me, James. We have so many more adventures to embark upon, so many more stories to share." Memories I wanted to make with him flowed through me, a river of love and devotion that surged with each beat of my heart. "I want you to marry me in the ruins of some long-forgotten castle, and I want to make little vampire babies with you."

I leaned in close, and my lips brushed against his, their warmth seeping into his icy skin. "I want to share my soul with you. Will you take me, let me be your Serenity?"

It was then that I felt it, a connection that transcended the physical realm. The very core of who I was, my love, my life, my soul, lifted from my very essence and as if the threads of fate had woven us together in a tapestry of longing and passion. My soul became his. We were one. It was a bond unlike any other I had ever experienced, at once both powerful and delicate, like the intricate lacework I painstakingly crafted for my most treasured designs.

I deepened the kiss, and I could feel the essence of our love flowing between us, a tide of emotions that swelled with each passing moment. I held on to the memory of his laughter, the heat of his embrace in the throes of passion, and the feel of his fangs, drinking from me, making me as intoxicated on his love as the finest wine.

Please, James, I thought, willing him to hear the silent plea in my soul. "Let our shared soul find peace together. Be my Serenity too."

Slowly, ever so slowly, I felt a shift, a subtle change in the air as if the universe around us had gone quiet, waiting for his answer.

The chill that had once consumed James began to dissipate, replaced by a warmth similar to my own skin, that grew stronger with each passing second.

"Rose," he whispered, his voice barely more than a breath, but carrying within it the promise of hope, of healing, and of a love that would never fade. He murmured against my lips, the word barely more than a breath, but heavy with emotion, with the weight of everything we had been through together. "My Rose."

The cold, hard ground beneath me seemed a distant concern as I focused on the feel of James's lips against mine, their softness marred by the sharp sting of his fangs as they sliced through my own flesh. The taste of copper filled my mouth, mingling with the intoxicating flavor of him, and I knew that this was the moment that could save his life or condemn us both to oblivion.

Our eyes met, locked in a gaze that spoke volumes without the need for words, and I felt the first tentative pull of his fangs against my skin, drawing the blood from my body and into his own.

I pushed away the fear that had threatened to overwhelm me, focusing on the love that burned so brightly between us. "Let me be your Serenity."

His eyes fluttered shut as he drank, the sensation of our beings merging, knitting us together, enveloping us in warmth like the glow of a thousand suns. I felt it deep within me, a connection far beyond what we'd even had when we'd made love. The room fell away, leaving only the two of us suspended in our shared emotions, tethered to one another by a bond that grew ever stronger with each beat of our hearts.

"Enough," he whispered, breaking the kiss and pulling back just enough to look into my eyes. To my relief, I saw it there, a flicker of light returning to those beautiful dark depths, a spark of life that sent a thrill of joy coursing through me.

"Rose," he said, his voice steadier now, filled with wonder and gratitude. "You... saved me."

"Of course I did." My heart swelled with a fierce, protective love that felt bigger than anything else in the world. "You're my Soul's Serenity."

"And you're mine," he whispered, the words heavy with emotion, and as my soul continued to intertwine with him, melding together like the threads of a golden bond that tied us together and could never be broken.

The intensity made me tremble, and I couldn't help but feel vulnerable, as if my soul was laid bare before everyone here.

His hand found mine and he gripped my fingers tight in his.

"Can you sit up?" I asked, eager to see how much he had recovered.

"Let's find out." With a grunt of effort, James pushed himself into a seated position, his arm still wrapped around me for support. He glanced around the room and nodded at Gabriel and Ms. Primrose as if expecting to see his friends here by his side. James's face blanched when he spotted the new vampire who watched us from the shadows, his arms crossed over his broad chest.

I smiled at the vampire, and somehow, I knew the returning one he gave me was a rare one. But I liked how it tugged at the corners of his lips as he took in the scene before him.

There was relief in his eyes, a glimmer of hope that perhaps, one day, he, too, could find his own Serenity.

Before I could say as much, the vampire turned and walked right out into the sun, a few feet across the yard, and then, poof, he was gone in a puff of smoke. "Ooh, that's a fancy vamp trick. Who was that guy?"

Gabriel and James looked at each other like they'd just seen a ghost. Ms. Primrose reapplied her lipstick.

James interjected, his voice now steadier than before, "Perhaps you two could give us a moment? It seems, after all this, Rose and I have some... catching up to do."

"Of course," Gabriel replied, a knowing glint in his eye. He dipped his head, grabbed Ms. Primrose's hand and dragged her out of the shed, leaving James and me alone.

"Finally," James sighed, pulling me closer. "A moment of peace."

"Peace?" I raised an eyebrow, a mischievous grin spreading across my face. "I thought we were catching up."

"Ah, yes." His eyes darkened with desire, his fingertips tracing patterns on my skin. "There is much to catch up on, isn't there?"

"Indeed," I murmured, feeling a shiver run down my spine at his touch. My heart pounded in anticipation, our earlier fears and doubts fading away as we focused solely on one another.

As our gazes locked, the world around us ceased to

exist. It was just James and me, forever bound by love and sacrifice. We had faced unimaginable adversity and emerged stronger than ever before. Now, we would celebrate our connection in the most intimate way possible.

"Show me how much you've missed me," I whispered, my pulse racing as I leaned in to press my lips against his once more.

The kiss was slow and sensual, a dance of desire that left us both breathless. James gently pushed me back onto the soft earth, his body covering mine as we continued to explore one another. Our hands roamed freely, reacquainting ourselves with every curve, every scar, a testament to our shared journey.

"James," I breathed, my voice ragged as desire coursed through my veins. "Are you sure you're up for this? You were dead just a minute ago."

"Rose." He pressed his lips to my throat and dragged his fangs across my skin. "You just shared your soul with me. I've never felt better in all my hundreds of years."

He lifted me over him and shredded my shirt, then my pants, and it took him all of a second to divest me of my bra and panties.

Good thing I had that blood red cloak to throw on later.

"I need very much to taste you, Rose. Come up here and put that luscious cunt on my mouth."

He grabbed my hips and dragged me, not that I was kicking and screaming to say no, and sat me right down on his face.

I rode his lips like a very happy cowgirl. It wasn't like he was going to die again.

When I was so close to coming, I groaned and ground my hips on him. "Please, you know what I want. Bite me, James. Do it. Make me come."

The sharp sting of his fang slid into my pulsing clit, and I let out a long, low groan as my world went explosive with pleasure.

I was still shuddering from the effects of that orgasm when he flipped us both, climbed over me, and entered me, filling me completely, with my pussy still pulsing from that massive climax. He made love to me with long, slow strokes, peppering me with kisses and nips that drove me wild.

We moved together, lost in a world of sensation that transcended the act of sex, and became a sharing once again of my soul intertwining with the emptiness in him, now faded and filled. Our bodies intertwined, and I pulled his face to my neck, needing once again for him to take blood from me, and reconfirm our unbreakable bond that would last an eternity.

"James..." I gasped, feeling the pressure building within me, threatening to consume us both.

My name was a growl, his own control slipping. He sank his fangs into me, and it was as if time slowed to a crawl. This moment, our union, our love, this bond between us, it was all that mattered.

Together, we reached the peak of ecstasy, our cries of pleasure echoing for all to hear.

When we were both so spent we couldn't move even an inch, I lay wrapped in James's arms.

"I love you, James Vond. I'm not sure I've ever said that and figured you should probably know."

He chuckled and kissed the top of my head. "I did in fact know that, my Serenity. But I do love hearing it just the same. I will love you forever and always. While the words are delicious, I'd rather show you at least a dozen more times."

"Ooh. You did say vampires had great stamina. I think I'm going to enjoy that."

"I did get some advice somewhere along the way that said mates liked lots and lots of orgasms."

JAMES

The grand hall of Chillingham Castle loomed before us, its ancient walls emanating a sense of power and mystery. Rose leaned on me, her breaths mostly gasps as she looked around at the historical building as we made our way inside.

"James," Rose whispered, her eyes wide as she took in the imposing architecture of the Vampire Intelligence Agency's headquarters. "It's beautiful. And you're telling me that all the tourists who come here don't see half of it?"

"Nope, only those in the VIA, the immortals and very special humans like you." My voice was rough with pride. This was my world, and now, it was hers too.

The great oak doors swung open, revealing Ms. Primrose standing there, her seemingly unassuming demeanor at odds with the gravity of the situation. She smiled warmly at us, her eyes twinkling with a mischievous glint.

"Ah, James, Rose," she said, striding forward to meet

us. "I'm glad to see you made it back in one piece... more or less."

"Ms. Primrose," I nodded, holding Rose closer to me. I sensed her anxiety grow, her pulse quickening beneath my touch. We'd been summoned by V himself, and the balance of our futures were in his hands.

A notification on her computer dinged and she tilted her head. "He's ready for you, go on in."

"Thank you."

The doors swung open, and even though I'd been with the VIA for hundreds of years, this was a threshold I'd never crossed. The inner sanctum of the First Vampire himself, head of the Agency.

The vampire who stood behind the desk, looking through a pile of books was not what I expected. I'd seen this agent on half a dozen cases I worked, and yet I didn't know his name. This couldn't be V. He was as unassuming as any other vampire in the world.

That is, until we caught his attention, and I felt the full force of the one who had created my entire race.

Holy shit. I almost fell down on my knees under his presence and power. Rose just smiled and held out her hand to him.

"Oh, hi. Nice to see you again," she said as if she was greeting an old acquaintance.

V took her hand, his returning smile warm. "Ah, Rose. Your bravery and skill in rescuing Princess Mary of Orange and foiling the plot of Anna, the Bathory Assassin, have not gone unnoticed."

Rose blushed at the praise, and I couldn't help but feel a surge of pride on her behalf. I'd thrown an entire world of supernatural crazy at her in the span of less than a week, and she'd faced all of it head-on and emerged triumphant. She was truly remarkable.

"Couldn't have done it without James," she said, her tone light and jovial.

"Indeed," V agreed, his gaze lingering on her for a moment longer before turning to me. "You've both done exceptionally well. The Agency is fortunate to have you."

Uh. So, I wasn't getting fired, or excommunicated, or whatever V did to vampires who found their Serenity?

"Rose, your courage and resourcefulness have been nothing short of extraordinary," he said. "It is clear that you've earned a place among us."

Her eyes widened with a mix of disbelief and excitement. She glanced at me, as if looking for something—reassurance or permission, perhaps. I gave her a small nod, hoping to convey my support for whatever choice she made. After all, this was her journey as much as it was mine.

"Thank you, V," she stammered, her voice barely above a whisper. "I... I never imagined I could be a part of something like this."

She looked every bit the heroine who had just conquered her own fears and taken down an assassin in the process. I could feel the weight of V's words as he continued to praise her.

"Your actions speak for themselves, Rose," V replied, his voice gentle yet firm. "I'd like you to become one of VIA's permanent assets, working side by side with James on special missions, directly for me."

Special missions.

I'd heard of other vampires tapped for this division of VIA. Few ever saw them again. But I knew they were out there working their asses off, because I'd relied on their intel more than a time or two.

Rose's chest expanded and fell with each deep breath she took pondering her choice, her fingers entwined together with mine as if to keep herself grounded.

"James?" she finally asked, her voice the very opposite of tentative. "What do you think?"

This woman who had stormed into my life and irrevocably changed it was definitely something special. I would stand by her no matter what she decided she wanted to do. But I did hope she'd pick becoming an agent with me.

"Rose," I began, my voice low and steady, "I believe in you. I know you can do this. And I'll be with you every step of the way. If you want to do this, it will be a grand adventure for you and me."

Our gazes locked, and a flicker of determination ignited within her. It was that same fire that had first caught my attention, the spark that had drawn me to her like a moth to a flame.

"Alright," she said, her voice strong and confident. "I accept. On one condition. I get to bring my best friend Jorge into the know. I can't keep secrets from him, and I won't cut him out of my life."

"Excellent. I accept your condition. I have plans for young Jorge." V smiled, his eyes crinkling with genuine happiness. "Welcome to our society, Rose. Together, we'll face whatever challenges lie ahead and protect this world we've come to cherish."

"Rose, you have a perfect cover story," I said with a

grin. "A couture designer by day, and a spy by night. I can't think of anyone better suited for this world."

Her eyes sparkled with excitement, the initial hesitation slowly fading away. I could see her mind already racing with ideas, eagerly imagining the thrilling adventures that awaited us.

"Thank you." She smiled at me with such love and radiance, I almost threw her over my shoulder to carry her off and have my way with her. Almost.

V stepped forward, his smile turning serious. "Now, if you'll allow me, Rose, let me formally welcome you into our immortal world."

He produced a small box from within his coat pocket and opened it, revealing a pin in the shape of a bat with its wings outstretched. The intricate black and silver design matched my own, and shimmered in the dim light of his office, as if infused with an otherworldly power.

"Take this pin, Rose," V said, his voice solemn yet gentle. "Wear it as a symbol of your acceptance and newfound status among us."

As Rose reached out to accept the pin, I felt a strange sensation wash over me—a mix of anticipation and trepidation, knowing that our lives were about to change irrevocably. But as I glanced at the woman beside me, her eyes alight with determination, I knew that together, we were ready to face whatever challenges lay ahead.

"Ooh, accessories." Rose whispered, her fingers carefully closing around the pin. Rose's fingers trembled as she fastened the pin to the collar of her blouse. She looked over at me, a fire kindled in her eyes, and I knew, without any doubt, that she had found her place among us. "Thank you. I won't let you down."

"Of that, I have no doubt." V waved us away. "See Ms. Primrose for your first assignment. And tell her to send in Gabriel. I have an assignment I want him to take our young Silvanus on."

And so, with the weight of our shared destiny upon our shoulders, Rose and I left the grand hall hand in hand, ready to embrace the unknown and each other.

"James," she breathed, her voice steady with newfound confidence, "I feel a surge of power running through me, like I've tapped into something ancient and unyielding."

"Embrace it, Rose," I urged her gently, my own heart swelling with pride. "This is where you belong, and I am honored to stand by your side as we face this world together."

Our gazes locked, and for a moment, we were suspended in time, the weight of our shared destiny anchoring us to each other. The love that had blossomed between us was palpable, its tendrils weaving around our hearts, binding us closer than any mortal bond ever could.

As we stood there, wrapped in each other's presence, the grand hall seemed to fade away, leaving only the two of us in our sacred space. We leaned in, drawn together like magnets, our lips meeting in a tender kiss that promised a lifetime of devotion and passion.

"Whatever lies ahead," I vowed, pulling back slightly to look into her eyes, "we will face it together, hand in hand, heart to heart."

"Nothing can break us apart," Rose agreed, her voice filled with determination. "We are bound by love, and that, my dearest James, is the strongest force in this world—mortal or immortal."

With our promises exchanged and our hearts aligned, we stepped away from each other, a renewed sense of purpose coursing through our veins. The unknown may have loomed before us, but together, we were a force to be reckoned with - a pair forged in love, tempered by courage, and destined to be together, forever.

"James," she murmured, her cheeks flushed with emotion, "before all this happened, I never imagined that I would find someone like you, someone who sees me for who I truly am, who believes in my strengths and accepts my flaws."

"Rose," I whispered, my chest tightening at her words, "you have given me something I never thought possible for a creature like me, a reason to live, to hope, and to embrace the world anew."

I leaned in for a quick kiss, not wanting to start something we couldn't finish here in the castle where too many eyes watched. "Though I must admit, I never thought I'd meet a woman like you."

"Like me?" she inquired, raising an eyebrow.

"Beautiful, talented, and unafraid of the darkness within," I replied softly, my eyes locking onto hers.

"Ah, but James," she whispered, leaning in closer, "the darkness only makes the light shine brighter."

EPILOGUE - SILAS

I grinned and bared my fangs at the human lackey before me. Inhuman, lethal, cold as death itself. Seeing a vampire about to eat you was enough to scare most men.

Not this guy.

I'd blame that on the long and storied history of vampires in New Orleans. Not that we frequented the area, but don't tell all the authors who wanted to interview us.

Fine. He might think he wasn't scared of me. But he would be. One calculated punch to the nose to incapacitate him but not kill, coming up. I'd drag him into the field office for questioning. Then he'd know real fear. Unless, of course, he didn't fess up. Then he'd know death on a much more intimate basis.

I clenched my hand, prepared to knock him down, but he was ready, and his fist came straight for my face. I had to duck, narrowly avoiding his jab. Okay, not an ordinary human then. That was an interesting clue in the case.

The breeze from his punch mussed my hair as I slid beneath the blow. The bastard was fast, but I was faster. It's bad enough that this traitor was involved in a plot to kill His Majesty the King, but making me look anything less than absolutely fucking dapper was a crime against women I had yet to woo everywhere.

It would be so easy to simply tear his throat out, drink from him and know his thoughts, then kill him. But I was not my father. I snarled and swung around in a circle, faster than the human eye should be able to track, and moved to sweep his legs out from underneath him.

Bad guy lackey smirked and leapt into the air, clearing my attempt to knock him down by several inches. Bollocks. He was either a supernatural masking his true form or a human somehow altered and trained specifically to engage in combat with monsters like me. Either way, this fight just got much more fun.

I gave him the universal come at me hand gesture and then lunged, reaching for his throat. As quick as thought, he was gone, tearing up and out of the dirty, wet alley we fought in and toward the busy Bacchanalia known as Bourbon Street.

The door to the underground gambling den behind me still stood ajar. I debated going back to get Gabriel. Just when I'd decided not to, he peered out from the rickety doorframe at me, in his usual mentor knows best way.

Gabriel gestured at the empty alley that showed the signs of my struggle with Nameless Lackey. "Are you going to get the goon or what, Silvanus?"

He tilted his head at me lazily, like we had all the time in the world for a lesson in spycraft.

I flipped him off, and muttered, "He's heading into the public, come on."

Gabriel snorted, and I could practically hear his oncoming eyeroll. Not today, sir. I turned and sped up the alley after my prey. "Try to keep up, old man."

The fact that I was almost a thousand years younger than him was my constant companion on our missions together and gave me all the fodder I needed to poke at his impending retirement.

Gabriel called me something very ungentlemanly, and I snorted at his taunt. I harassed him for being as old as the First Vampire himself, and he regularly gave me an earful for being nothing but a playboy.

It wasn't my fault V wouldn't allow any vampire under the age of a hundred to join Vampire Intelligence. What else was I supposed to do in the last ninety-nine years besides amass my fortune then spend it on all the delicious women I loved to love?

I'd become particularly good at both endeavors. I'd be even better at protecting the Crown. Well, maybe not as good as I was at wooing women to my bed and making them come until they didn't know their names or mine.

I wove in and out of the pedestrians weaving about from bar to bar. It was a skill to do in a way that was both quick and yet unnoticeable, but this was what we trained for at the Castle. I slid between and amongst the mortals, catching little snippets of their conversations as I passed. Nameless Lackey raced ahead of me, and the tingle of the frenzy that came only when in pursuit of prey zipped through my arteries and veins.

Damn if I didn't love the chase.

My father's own prey-chasing frenzies led to some of his greatest, most daring feats. Not that it would matter if I, too, leapt from a moving train to the bottom of Reichenbach Falls, covertly assassinated King Alexander of Greece, or famously escaped from the Nazis at Dresden.

I would never be him. Never as good, as fast, as powerful. As needed.

No, my service to King Charles was another story altogether. In my training for the agency, I had thus far rolled in the mud with the Baskervilles's household dog, smoked one of Churchill's cigars, and somehow ended up naked in the Tower of London wearing only the Crown Jewels on my—ahem—crown jewels.

Gabriel had photographic evidence of every last one. He liked to show those shots to me whenever he felt I was a bit too mouthy. So, basically weekly.

My first real case for the storied but secret Vampire Intelligence Agency was turning out to be a doozy.

The frenetic energy of the hunt rose in my veins, bubbling through me. I moved faster, slipping through the crowd after my quarry. My senses took over as the primal instinct increased, the thrill of pursuit making me more beast than man. The humans around us bled into nothing more than gray streaks in my vision. I saw only my prey.

I closed in and could smell the tang of fear in the man's sweat. So he was human. Interesting. His eyes flicked to me, widened for an instant, then he pushed himself to move faster. He shoved his way through the foot traffic and then veered straight into a crowded club booming with earsplitting music.

Splendid. This was to be the site of my first agency sanctioned showdown. Even single-handedly foiling the plot to kill the King wasn't going to be good enough to impress Gabriel or V, because public battles weren't dignified enough to satisfy VIA's sense of propriety.

Gabriel was an old school spy, but a modern vampire. The tuxedo, the gadget-filled car, the horde of women that he fed from, bedded, and then erased their memories. He was suave and somehow charming, even though I knew he was a cold-blooded monster, just like me.

I was young to his anciently old, inexperienced to his sophistication, fumbling and awkward, skating through training by the skin of my pointy teeth, to his total and complete debonaire professionalism. Yet I was the one carrying around the name of Silvanus, the legacy of the greatest hero the VIA has ever known.

Today was going to be my day, or rather, night, damn it. I tracked down this lead all the way to America, set up the meet at the underground poker game, and now I was the one just minutes away from snatching this bad guy off the streets and interrogating the living daylights out of him. I'd make him spill everything about everyone he'd ever met, and I'd save the King.

Then I'd be the hero for a change, instead of always being the disappointing son of a gun.

I sensed Gabriel behind me, but he was slower than I was in my blood-frenzied state. I'd capture the baddie while he just watched and have the confession sucked out of this runt by the time Gabriel caught up to us. My lips curled in triumph, my fangs pressing into my bottom lip.

I'd have the confession already if he hadn't run. The fact that he'd run, even though he could fight, meant he had some intel that would be devastating if caught. He'd fled into the crowded French Quarter streets in order to slow me. But the blood and battle lust were already in me, and I wasn't going to settle for anything other than the hot wash of this villain's blood washed down with a nice beignet and a cafe au lait. I could practically taste the accolades already, feel it singing in my veins.

Right as the man came within arm's reach again, the scent of something even more enticing than blood and victory hit me square in the empty place inside where my absent soul gaped. I tried to shake it off, but in the blur of humanity, one individual stood out in full color. I lost control and slammed full body into the throng of dancing tourists.

"Woohoo, mosh pit!" Humans squealed and screamed around me, crashing into each other and me to the beat of the music.

I allowed them to throw themselves at me and I scanned the room for the human who'd snagged my attention away from my prey. No, not any human, a woman.

What the hell? Sure, I loved the pursuit of a beautiful woman and a tryst between the sheets. But never had it interfered with the hunt or especially my training for the agency. This had to be a ploy by whomever that lackey was working for.

And of course, now I'd lost sight of the prey. I pushed

my way out of the circle of crashing dancers, opening my senses to find the trail again. My attention went immediately to a group of women gathered around a single high-top table in the far corner of the room. Even from here I could smell the delicious scent of their blood, hear the intense beating of their hearts.

None of them was her. The one whose color filled my black and white world.

At least one of them was involved in this conspiracy to distract me from the escaped lackey though. The same colors swirled around them. I approached the table, intent on using a bit of mind allure to interrogate them so they'd tell me who this mysterious woman was that they were working for.

The party-girl closest held a cupcake aloft and pointed it at me. "Ew, creep. Take your stalker vibes somewhere else."

Wisps of the powerful spell swirled around her hand in sunshiny golds and yellows. The scent of dark chocolate wafted toward me. I didn't even like sweets. Unless of course it was the sweet nectar of a lover's blood. A coven of witches or perhaps succubae out looking for their own sex and blood temptations.

A second party-girl turned, also holding a cupcake with the same golden, sparkling wisps dripping from the treat. "Shush your face, he's not a stalker, he's too hot."

The sweet spell swirled around her, wafting toward me. My fangs ached and my mouth watered, but not for any of these women. They were nothing more than mere humans. Good for a hot fling, or even a fun snack, but not dangerous, useful in this mission, or what the spell had me craving.

No, this was beyond any mere craving. My mouth went from watering to parched in the absence of the one thing that would fulfill this need. I snatched the cupcake from the starry-eyed woman nearest me and inhaled the delicious scent, pulling the bit of sunshine into my very essence. There had to be a clue in the magic that would lead me to the supernatural being attempting to thwart this mission.

The spell already had its hold on me, more exposure to it wouldn't make a difference. Perhaps a taste would reveal information to guide me to its creator. Whoever had placed this distraction between me and the lackey would be a much better hot lead.

I dipped my tongue into the decadent frosting, waiting for the sickly-sweet sugar to invade my tastebuds. Instead, the rich chocolate went straight to my head as if I was sucking on the most delicious of throats. I had to have more. In several bites, I inhaled the cake, barely taking time to savor the flavors.

"Whoa," the woman before me looked at her friends, all of them wide-eyed. "I was going to go all Karen on you for taking my expensive ass cupcake, but this is like food porn and actual porn at the same time. Wanna do that to me later? Or, like, right now?"

I grabbed her by the arm and pulled her to me and with my other hand, snagged another cupcake from the next nearest woman. I shoved that one into my mouth too, not caring for manners or propriety. "Where did you get these? Who gave them to you?"

"Silvanus." Gabriel sauntered across the room towards us, the dancers parting like a red sea of bodies doing his bidding. "You've got a bit of chocolate there."

He pointed to my face and the front of my shirt, and the girl looked up at me like a scared but enamored chocolate-covered bunny caught in the trap of a seductive monster.

I released the slip of a thing and eyed both the crumbs I'd dribbled all over her, and the rest of the cupcakes on the table. There was no resisting. I grab another and another, one in each hand, shoved one into my mouth, still unsatisfied, then pointed at Gabriel. "Stand back. This is a powerful spell."

Gabriel raised his phone and took a picture. "Is it? Looks like chocolate buttercream on a moist Victoria sponge with ganache drizzled over the top. I'm sure I saw that exact recipe on the finale of Bake-Off last week."

"Do you not see the wisps of sunshine magic swirling around them? This is a trap, or a distraction to throw us off the scent."

"All I see is you making a mess of both yourself and these lovely ladies." He gave them a wink, and with it, a push into their minds that would make them forget they'd ever seen the two of us. "Excellent job, Silas. I'll let HQ know we lost the trail."

Bloody hell. I knew I was in trouble when he used my first name.

He was right. I'd lost the lackey. But there would be no convincing me that this wasn't a break in the case. We were dealing with magically enhanced humans and a spell that had stopped me dead in my tracks. That was a hell of a lot more than we'd known before tonight.

The plot to assassinate the king on his upcoming visit to the United States was no mere human looking to become famous.

Fleming would probably be able to analyze the chocolate and the spell to come up with a preventative or antidote. I took one more cupcake from the table, leaving just one in the box. Might as well take that one too. And the box.

"Look," I held the box aloft showing Gabriel another clue as I sank my teeth into another cupcake. "A bold spellcaster to print their name on the container. We'll track them down and interrogate them."

The name of my new nemesis was now emblazoned on my mind. I was coming for the villain known as Winn-Dixie.

NEED JUST a little more of James and Rose?

I've written a special bonus chapter! Grab it when you join my Curvy Connection email.

READY FOR THE next book in the series where Silas meets his Soul's Serenity?

Grab *The Vampire Who Loved Me* now!

ACKNOWLEDGMENTS

Thank you to Michael Hauge for helping me work through the plot and characters for my crazy idea to write James Bond vampires. I'm so very grateful you asked me if I would date this guy… because in the original version the answer was no.

But I would definitely do this James.

Special thanks to Becca Mysoor, the Fairy Plotmother for recogonizing that I was starting this series in the wrong place, and helping me come up with something new from scratch that matched the real vision I had for my curvy girls and vampires. The series is better because of you.

Hugs to my mastermind group: JL Madore, Krystal Shannon, Claudia Burgoa, and Bri Blackwood for giving me such lovely achievers to compete with so I actually get something done.

More appreciation than I can ever express to my assistant Michelle Ziegler for always believing I can actually do the crazy things I set out to do and for supporting me even when she thinks I've gone off the deep end.

My Amazeballs Facebook group is so much of the reason I keep writing and I look forward to logging onto the FaceSpace every day and seeing what kind of fun and games we've got going on!

Big thanks to my proofreader, Chrisandra. She probably hates commas as much as I do now. All the remaining errors are all my fault. I'm sure I screwed it up somewhere.

I'm ever grateful to Becca Syme for telling me I'm worth fighting for when I'm sure I've effed up my book and my career. I swear one of these days I'm going to realize it's a problem with the story, and not my brain.

I am so very grateful to have readers who will join my on my crazy book adventures where there will ALWAYS be curvy girls getting happy ever afters!

Without all of you, I wouldn't be able to feed my cats (or live the dream of a creative life!)

Thank you so much to all my Patreon Book Dragons!

An enormous thanks to my Official Biggest Fans Ever. You're the best book dragons a curvy girl author could ask for~

Thank you so much for all your undying devotion for me and the characters I write. You keep me writing (almost) every day.

Hugs and Kisses and Signed Books and Swag for you from me! I am so incredibly grateful for each of you and am awed by your support. I read every single one of your messages and replies to the Patreon posts and it gives me all the motivation in the world to keep writing!

- Alida H.
- Cherie S.
- Dale W.
- Danielle T.
- Daphine G.
- Jessica W.
- Katherine M.
- Kelli W.
- Marilyn C.
- Mari G.
- Melissa L.
- Rosa D.
- Bridget M.
- Stephanie F.
- Stephanie H.

Shout out to my Official VIP Fans!
Extra Hugs and to you ~

- Anna P.
- Barbara B.
- Jeanette M.
- Corinne A.
- Hannah P.
- Jeanette M.
- Kerrie M.
- Natasha H.
- Sandra B.
- Sarah M.
- Tracy L.
- Frania G.

ALSO BY AIDY AWARD

Dragons Love Curves

Chase Me

Tease Me

Unmask Me

Bite Me

Cage Me

Baby Me

Defy Me

Surprise Me

Dirty Dragon

Crave Me

Dragon Love Letters - Curvy Connection Exclusive

Slay Me

Play Me

Merry Me

The Black Dragon Brotherhood

Tamed

Tangled

Twisted

Fated For Curves

A Touch of Fate

A Tangled Fate

A Twist of Fate

Alpha Wolves Want Curves

Dirty Wolf

Naughty Wolf

Kinky Wolf

Hungry Wolf

Grumpy Wolves

Filthy Wolf

The Fate of the Wolf Guard

Unclaimed

Untamed

Undone

Undefeated

Claimed by the Seven Realms

Protected

Stolen

Crowned

By Aidy Award and Piper Fox

Big Wolf on Campus

Cocky Jock Wolf

Bad Boy Wolf

Heart Throb Wolf

Hot Shot Wolf

Contemporary Romance by Aidy Award

The Curvy Love Series

Curvy Diversion

Curvy Temptation

Curvy Persuasion

The Curvy Seduction Saga

Rebound

Rebellion

Reignite

Rejoice

Revel

ABOUT THE AUTHOR

Aidy Award is a curvy girl who kind of has a thing for stormtroopers. She's also the author of the popular Curvy Love series and the hot new Dragons Love Curves series. She writes curvy girl erotic romance, about real love, and dirty fun, with happy ever afters because every woman deserves great sex and even better romance, no matter her size, shape, or what the scale says.

Read the delicious tales of hot heroes and curvy heroines come to life under the covers and between the pages of Aidy's books. Then let her know because she really does want to hear from her readers.

Connect with Aidy on her website. www.AidyAward.com get her Curvy Connection, and join her Facebook Group - Aidy's Amazeballs.

Printed in Great Britain
by Amazon